For Joe Gyorffi,
who awakened my interest in the Titanic,
and in memory of the over 1,500 men, women, and
children who died in the Atlantic ice fields,
April 15, 1912

TITANIC CROSSING

Barbara Williams

AN
APPLE
PAPERBACK

SCHOLASTIC INC.
New York Toronto London Auckland Sydney

ISBN 0-590-94464-9

31 30 29 28 27 26

0 1 2/0

Printed in the U.S.A.   40
First Scholastic printing, January 1997

TITANIC
CROSSING

One

Albert Trask was going home. To Washington. On the *Titanic.*

He felt like jumping hurdles. He felt like singing. He felt like shouting at the top of his lungs so his voice would echo and re-echo against these high-ceilinged walls of Waterloo Station. *Good-bye, London! You can have your soot. And your fog. And your old cricket games. You can have your know-it-all Miss Harcher!*

A tapping sound beside him interrupted his joyous farewell. Six-year-old Virginia was stamping her foot. "I don't want to go," she complained. She had that sour look on her face again, Albert noticed. If she weren't careful, she'd grow up to be just as dried-up and pinched-looking as Miss Harcher.

Uncle Claybourne stiffened and Mother turned away. Neither of them spoke.

3

But Albert was too excited to let his little sister rile him the way she sometimes did. Instinctively he reached into his pocket and with two fingers stroked the watch Father had given him that last day before he died. Even though he couldn't see the watch, even though he hadn't opened the cover, Albert knew what was engraved inside:

> To Mason from Katherine,
> My love forever,
> 6–8–98.

He pulled his hand from his pocket and pressed a fist against the sudden tightness in his chest. It was the sensation he always felt when he thought of Father lying in that bed, his face gray as cardboard and his golden hair spread out like an Oriental fan. "Albert, you must be the man of the family now. You must take care of your mother and little sister."

Albert took a deep breath and bent down toward Ginny. "Remember our house?"

"No."

"It's bigger than the flat in London. And you don't have to climb two flights of steps to get to it."

"I don't care."

"Lots prettier too. You have rosebuds on the wallpaper in your room at home. And a canopied bed with ruffles on it."

"I don't care."

"And the zoo in Rock Creek Park is only a mile away. We can walk there together," Albert suggested. "Anytime you like."

"There's a zoo here. Miss Harcher's going to take me. She said so."

"But she hasn't, has she? Do you know why?"

"N-n-no."

"Because London is always cold and rainy. It's no fun to go to the zoo in the rain."

He thought about the London rain and cold. The bleak air filtered through his coat and gloves, flailing his skin and paralyzing his bones. How could anyone want to stay in damp, bitter London when they could go to Washington?

"Well, why can't we take Miss Harcher to Washington, then?" Virginia whined.

Albert rolled his eyes toward the high rafters. He couldn't imagine taking their ugly old tutor anywhere, especially to Washington. That old biddy may have fooled a six-year-old like Virginia, but Albert was thirteen. He knew what a hypocrite Miss Harcher was, grinning at him with her yellow teeth and fawning over the sketches in his art tablet, when she was just waiting for the chance to tell Mother he hadn't memorized his declensions and needed stricter discipline.

Ginny tugged at Mother's arm. "How come we can't take Miss Harcher?"

Mother didn't answer right away, so Albert took another deep breath and tried again. "You get to take Elizabeth to America instead." He nodded toward the porcelain doll Ginny was carrying. It was a splendid doll from Harrods that had cost nearly as much as Albert's new three-piece gray suit with long trousers. He could hardly wait for dinner tonight on shipboard, when he would wear long pants for the first time.

"I want to take Miss Harcher too," Virginia wailed.

"Hush, dear," Mother said at last, "or Uncle Clay will think you don't love the new doll Grandmother Trask bought you." Mother's words sounded pleasant enough, but Albert could tell by the way she avoided looking at Uncle Clay when she spoke that she was still upset at him. She hadn't forgiven him for coming to London or for telling the rest of them that they had to go home.

Now she bent toward Virginia, spreading a gentle scent of lilac cologne. "Maybe we'll come back to London and see Miss Harcher again sometime."

Uncle Clay frowned. "Katherine!"

"Well, maybe we will," Mother said, standing straight. "After I report to Mother Trask and she sees that England hasn't—hasn't *defiled* any of us, maybe she'll urge us to come back here."

"And maybe not," said Uncle Clay. "Your traveling costume is very—uh—modern, Kitty, but perhaps Mother would consider black more appropriate."

Albert studied Mother's outfit. He thought she looked very nice—beautiful, even. Uncle Clay should be proud to be seen with such a stylish lady. On her head was an elegant wide-brimmed hat with a lavender plume. Over her shoulders was a knee-length black sealskin stole. With her purple lamb's wool suit, Mother looked every bit as fashionable as the mannequins Albert had seen at Harrods. Like Virginia's doll and Albert's new suit, the fur stole had been purchased at London's famous department store by Uncle Clay on behalf of Grandmother Trask.

Virginia patted Mother's arm. "When?"

Ignoring Ginny, Mother faced Uncle Claybourne, her cheeks reddened, her voice shaking with emotion.

"Mercy, Clay. This is 1912. Even Mother Trask can't expect a thirty-three-year-old woman to spend the rest of her life in mourning."

"When?" Virginia repeated.

"No, but it's customary for a widow to wear black for a year," Uncle Clay told Mother, combing his blond mustache with two gloved fingers. Then he turned rigidly to study his other hand, which was resting on an umbrella wound tight as a cane. "It's only been seven months, you know."

"Nearly eight."

"Mother says black makes her look fallow," Virginia explained.

"Sallow, dear," Mother said, acknowledging Ginny at last.

The humor of Virginia's mistake wasn't lost on Uncle Claybourne. His mouth twitched into a bitter smile.

From the petit point satchel which hung from one arm, Mother pulled an opened box of biscuits. "Albert, why don't you take Ginny outside and see if there are any pretty birds on the platform you can feed?"

Ginny danced up and down. "Oh yes, Bertie. Let's go feed the birds."

Albert shifted his weight, uncertain about how to respond. He'd already tried to distract Virginia. Twice. Hadn't Mother noticed? And why couldn't Ginny feed the birds herself? If they had any time to spare before they caught the train, he'd rather get out his art tablet and try to sketch the interesting architecture of this waiting room.

"Albert—" Mother insisted.

Albert shrugged. If he could keep his pesky little sister

out of Mother's way for a while, he thought, maybe she and Uncle Clay could relax and settle their differences so everyone could enjoy the trip home.

"Yes, ma'am." He turned to Virginia. "Come on." Albert took his sister's hand and headed toward the huge glass doors that separated the waiting room from the platform.

Virginia skipped at his side, the soles of her new patent leather shoes tappity-tapping on the linoleum of the huge room. It was weird—really weird—how quickly Ginny's moods could shift. A person just had to know the right things to suggest to her.

A gust of cold air hit Albert's face as he opened the door. It stank of train oil, grease, and the usual London soot. But the pigeons didn't seem to notice. Through the gray mist Albert could see the outlines of several of them walking on the station platform. Another was perched on the tall pedestal clock.

Setting her doll on the concrete, Virginia reached with both hands. "Give me some biscuits!"

Albert unwrapped two cookies and handed them to her. "Don't yell. You'll scare the birds away."

"*I'm not yelling!*" Ginny shrieked. She crumpled the shortbread in her small fists and scattered the crumbs. "Ooh, look!" she cried as the pigeons dived for the food. She skipped back and forth to watch them. "Give me some more biscuits."

He unwrapped two more for her and kept a third one for himself. Chewing, he watched as she scattered more crumbs.

"Give me some more!" Ginny squealed.

"I can't. The biscuits are gone."

"Let me see!" Virginia reached for his pocket, but Albert jerked away. *R-r-r-rip!*

Albert studied the flap of houndstooth material hanging from his jacket. "Now see what you've done. I won't be able to get this fixed on the ship."

"It wasn't my fault. You shouldn't have moved."

"Can't you even say you're sorry? Mother packed up all my other old suits to give them away before we left London. This is the only one I brought."

"It is not. You have the new suit Grandmother bought you."

"But that's to wear at night. For dinner. It has long trousers."

"Wel-l-l. You said you wanted to wear long pants all the time now, anyway."

It was true. A month ago, for his birthday, Albert had asked Mother for a suit with long trousers. But instead she'd taken him out to dinner and the theater, to see the play *Man and Superman*. It was Grandmother who somehow understood how important it was to him to wear long trousers after he turned thirteen.

But on a fancy ship like the *Titanic* he couldn't wear the same suit day and evening for the whole crossing, even if it did have long trousers and made him look grown up. People would think he slept in it. He wondered if the pocket could be pinned until they got home.

Albert scowled at his sister. "We better go find Mother." He picked up Virginia's doll and handed it to her. "Here. Don't forget Elizabeth."

As Albert opened the big door for Ginny, a child with wispy hair and wearing a long coat pointed toward Albert and Virginia. "Look, Mummy. Birdies."

At first Albert thought the child had heard Virginia call him *Bertie* earlier and was repeating the name. But no, three pigeons had followed Albert and Ginny through the doorway and were now trapped inside Waterloo Station.

Good grief.

"Shoo," said Albert, holding the door open for the birds and swinging his free arm in a wide arc. "Shoo," he repeated, but the birds hopped farther inside the station.

Several people had gathered to watch the birds, including two boys just younger than Albert. The pigeons strutted.

"Does anyone have any bread or biscuits?" Albert asked. "I think I could catch them if I had some crumbs."

"I'll catch them," offered one of the boys. He lunged suddenly, but the birds were faster. One of them fluttered to the newspaper kiosk where large placards announced the day's news: Protesters Demonstrate in Ulster. End of Coal Strike Means Jobs for Factory and Ship Workers. The other birds flew high above the people's heads, to the uppermost area of the lofty waiting room.

Albert bit his lip, watching.

Then, from the kiosk, the third pigeon flew up to join its companions, and overhead the three of them soared gracefully back and forth and around, as if the warm station were where they belonged.

Suddenly a thud echoed through the room. One of the pigeons had sailed into a window, mistaking it for open space. It fell to the ground, lying stunned.

"Bertie!" screamed Virginia. "Don't let him die! Save him!"

Albert reached for the bird, but it limped to its feet and fluttered up to the kiosk. Now all three birds panicked.

With a great swishing of wings they flew crazily this way and that through the terminal. Albert watched anxiously. There was no way he could calm the birds enough to lure them outside without food of some kind.

Virginia raced back to Mother and Uncle Clay. "Mummy! Mummy! Don't let the birds die!"

But Mother wasn't interested in birds. She was still arguing with Uncle Clay. "You tricked me," she was saying to him. "You said we'd be traveling in first class."

Standing tall, Uncle Clay rested both hands on the curved handle of his umbrella. "That was before I purchased your stole and those other gifts. Afterward it seemed foolish to spend all the money Mother had given me just so we could travel in first class."

"I didn't ask you for any stole!" Mother raged.

Uncle Claybourne shrugged.

"The birdies!" Ginny cried, tugging at Mother's arm.

"Hush, dear. Your uncle and I are talking." Mother turned back to Uncle Clay, her cheeks the color of boiled shrimp. "The only reason I agreed to come with you was because you said we'd be sailing with Harry Gordon, the theatrical producer. You know one doesn't 'sail with' someone who's riding in a different class. We'll never even see Mr. Gordon and those other people you said would be traveling in first class."

Uncle Clay combed his mustache with his fingers. "I think maybe you agreed to come with me because Mama threatened to change the trust fund if you didn't."

Mother glared at Uncle Clay, shaking her head so violently that the handbag and satchel hooked over her arms swung like two pendulums. "She's trying to control me! She has no right to do that!"

"I know Mason's death was hard on you, Kitty. But you've never understood that it was hard on her too. And then to have you run off with her two grandchildren, the only ones she'll probably ever have, nearly destroyed her. The only way she felt she'd ever be able to see them regularly was to threaten to cut off your annuity if you refused to raise Albert and Virginia in America."

Mother clenched her hands, breathing hard.

Virginia used the silence to tug at Uncle Claybourne's trousers. *"You've got to help the birds!"*

His irritation exploding, Uncle Clay slapped at the small hand wrinkling his trousers. "Stop that, you obstreperous child! Have you no manners at all?"

Virginia gasped, then suddenly dissolved in tears, burying her face in Mother's skirt.

"Ginny, Ginny, it's all right," Mother said soothingly, bending over to stroke Virginia's hair. Then she looked up at Uncle Claybourne. "Don't you ever touch her again. Or Albert either. Ever. Do you hear?"

"All aboard! All aboard!" called a voice. *"Boat train for Southampton now leaving from track twelve."*

"Come along, Kitty," Uncle Claybourne said stiffly. "Take Virginia's hand, Albert."

"The birdies," Virginia wailed.

Albert reached for her hand. "They'll be all right. Someone will let them out," he assured her, confident he spoke the truth.

His mother and sister would be all right too, once they got to Washington, he thought.

Washington. They were going home, where he would have friends again. School friends. He could almost see himself playing baseball with them. He could almost taste the Sunday dinners that he would have at Grandmother Trask's country home in McLean, with the silverware gleaming beside the china plates and the table piled with Mattie Lou's wonderful-smelling dishes.

Holding Ginny's hand, he hurried to catch up with Mother and Uncle Claybourne, the excitement inside him steamy and swelling, like Mattie Lou's corn soufflé baking in Grandmother's oven.

TWO

Mother wasn't speaking to Uncle Claybourne.

She stood up from the bench seat facing the one Albert and his uncle were sitting on, removed Virginia's hat, and laid it carefully on the luggage rack above her head, ignoring Uncle Clay as if he were invisible. Next she removed her own hat, gloves, and stole and arranged them in a neat pile before setting them on the luggage rack too. Albert's cap and Uncle Claybourne's bowler were already resting on their seat between them, but Mother didn't offer to place them out of the way. Instead, she tucked her handbag and petit point satchel on her own seat and from the latter took a silver-handled hairbrush. "Here, Ginny, your hair's messed up. You want to look nice when we get on the ship, don't you?"

Virginia shrugged as if she didn't particularly care one way or the other, but Mother removed the ribbon from

Ginny's hair, slowly brushing the tangles and rewinding the ringlets around her index finger.

Albert watched the grace with which Mother worked. He wondered if Virginia, who was always bumping into things, would ever move like Mother or have her beauty. Virginia's face was round, and her lips, though pretty enough, drooped at the corners, even when she wasn't sulky or out of sorts. Blond and blue-eyed, she lacked the dramatic coloring of Mother's black hair and violet eyes. But their foreheads were alike, high and broad, and their heads rested on similar long, stately necks.

Mother retied Virginia's bow, pulling and primping the loops until the wide ribbon seemed like an oversized butterfly ready for flight. Then Mother put the hairbrush back in the satchel and removed an illustrated children's book. "Shall I read you some nursery rhymes?"

Virginia nodded and snuggled closer. Mother began reading:

> *Pussycat, pussycat,*
> *Where have you been?*
> *I've been to London*
> *To see the Queen.*
> *Pussycat, pussycat,*
> *What did you there?*
> *I frightened a little mouse*
> *Under the chair.*

Uncle Claybourne shifted in his seat as if the sound of Mother's voice disturbed his concentration, but he continued reading the paper he'd purchased from a newsboy selling them on the train.

Huddling with Virginia, Mother continued reading:

> *Three wise men of Gotham,*
> *Went to sea in a bowl,*
> *And if the bowl had been stronger,*
> *My song had been longer.*

"I say," Virginia complained in a tone she'd picked up from Miss Harcher. "That's a silly poem."

"Why do you think that?"

"Anyone knows a bowl would break if people climbed into it. You shouldn't go to sea in a silly little bowl. You should go in a fine ship, like the *Titanic*. Albert says the *Titanic* is the finest ship in the world. He says it's made so it can't sink."

"Albert should know." Mother spoke wearily. "He's been reading about nothing else ever since we came to England."

"Read me a *good* poem," Ginny coaxed. "Read me one I'll like."

"All right. How about this one?"

> *An angel came as I lay in bed;*
> *I will give you wings—the angel said;*
> *I will give you wings that you may fly*
> *To the country of Heaven above the sky.*
>
> *My beautiful angel flew away,*
> *He came not again by night or by day;*

Angels are busy with many things,
And he has forgotten to send the wings.

Virginia's eyelids looked heavy. The family had left their Kensington flat at 5:30 A.M. in order to reach Waterloo Station on time, and no one had had enough sleep last night. Mother shifted the objects on their seat so Virginia could lie down, her head in Mother's lap. Then she opened her satchel again and took out the thick Thomas Hardy novel Miss Harcher had given her for a going-away present.

Albert wished Mother would put the book down, that Uncle Clay would put his newspaper down. He wished everyone would talk to one another, the way families were supposed to when they were going on an exciting trip.

Never mind, he told himself. He had a spot by the window. Now was his chance to see a bit of the English countryside that Mother had never wanted to visit. "But we haven't seen all of London yet!" she'd always say. "There's so much to do in London!"

Outside, the sun was pushing through the morning haze, bathing the slate rooftops in deep orange. The train rattled through the suburbs where a deliveryman had stopped his horse-drawn wagon to remove a heavy milk churn. Farther along, an iceman was toting a cake of ice hoisted over his shoulder by sturdy tongs. An old woman wearing a heavy sweater was kneeling by her garden, spading the soil between lavender crocuses and yellow daffodils.

On the train sped. Faster and faster.

The lampposts disappeared, and houses grew farther apart. Hedgerows were taller. Slate roofs gave way to thatch. The train wheels clicked on their track. *Wash-ing-ton, Wash-ing-ton, Wash-ing-ton.*

Without warning, the train slowed to a stop. Virginia stirred on Mother's lap and sat up. "Are we there yet?"

"Not yet, dear. Go back to sleep."

"If we aren't there, why did we stop?"

"To let on more passengers, I suppose."

"Where are we?"

Mother looked out the window at the name on the station. "This is Reading. We're about halfway to Southampton. Why don't you lie down again and go back to sleep?"

"I don't need to go to sleep. I need to go to the loo."

"Don't say *loo*, dear. It isn't nice."

"Miss Harcher says *loo.*"

"Well, in our family we say *ladies' room.*"

"I need to go to the ladies' room."

Mother put away her novel and picked up her purse. "All right. Come on." She took Virginia by the hand and led her down the aisle.

As they disappeared, Albert felt a hand on his arm. "Albert, I need to talk to you."

Albert looked up at his uncle, feeling grown up and important. "Yes, sir. You know, I'm glad you came to get us, sir. I'm really happy to be going back to Washington. And I'm sorry about Ginny. She's only six, you know, and sometimes she acts really spoil—uh, cranky. I know she's upsetting Mother, but they'll—"

"Wel-l-l, yes."

Albert suddenly realized it wasn't Virginia's bad behavior that was troubling Uncle Claybourne, and he felt embarrassed for speaking out of turn. He fidgeted with the torn pocket on his jacket, waiting for his uncle to explain whatever was on his mind.

"Umm—How well do you know Zora LaRue?"

Albert sat up stiffly, not knowing what to say. Mother had specifically told him not to discuss Zora LaRue with Uncle Clay, but it was hard to avoid a direct question. "Zora LaRue?" he repeated, stalling. "Not too well, I suppose."

"Hmm," said Uncle Claybourne. "I've been told that you see her rather often—that she and your mother spent a great deal of time together in London."

Even though Albert didn't like Zora LaRue much—she was a silly woman who smoked cigarettes and used too much paint on her face and had opinions about everything—he felt it his duty to defend Mother. "Well, Miss LaRue was the only person Mother knew in London before we came here. They were roommates, you know, a long time ago. When they went to the Maryland Institute. Before Mother met Father."

"What do you think about Zora LaRue?"

Albert cleared his throat. "I don't know much about her. You should ask Mother."

"But it's your opinion I care about. Don't you have an opinion?"

Of course he had an opinion, but Albert knew it would be disloyal to Mother to discuss Miss LaRue at all. He leaned forward in his seat, straining to see down the aisle. Why didn't Mother and Virginia return from the ladies' room? "I guess I haven't thought much about her."

"Do you know she's an actress?"

How could anyone not know Miss LaRue was an actress? Mother had taken him three times to the theater to see Miss LaRue as Nora in *A Doll's House* by that Mr. Ibsen. Mother had loved the play each time, but Albert thought it was dopey—all about a silly woman who gets tired of having nice clothes and a beautiful house, so she suddenly packs up and leaves her husband and children. "Yessir."

"How do you feel about your mother spending her time with an actress?"

Mother not only spent her time with an actress, she wanted to *be* an actress. She talked about it all the time. She'd even tried out for a small part Miss LaRue had told her about. "I don't know," Albert said.

"Albert, do you know actresses are—fast?"

"Fast, sir?"

Uncle Claybourne paused for an instant, apparently trying to choose his words carefully. "Some women who work for a living, Albert, especially actresses, have—uh—advanced ideas. Dangerous ideas. Like this suffragette thing Zora LaRue is mixed up with. Do you know she believes women should be as free to come and go as men are? That they should have the right to vote?"

Of course Albert knew those things. He'd listened to Miss LaRue's crazy ranting a million times. "She's a suffragette?" he asked.

"Yes, there was an article all about it in the Washington newspaper just last month. It upset your grandmother to realize your mother was seeing Zora LaRue in London." Uncle Claybourne folded his newspaper and leaned close, speaking in a whisper. "Do you know Miss LaRue is divorced?"

"Uh—yessir."

For an instant Uncle Claybourne covered his mouth

with his hand, as if he were going to cough. But he only cleared his throat. "Do you approve of divorce, Albert?"

"I don't know much about it, sir. Miss LaRue is the first person I've ever met who's divorced."

"No one in the Trask family has ever been divorced."

"No, sir."

"Your grandmother doesn't approve of divorce."

"I suppose not, sir."

Uncle Clay combed his mustache with the blunt ends of two fingers, a habit that was beginning to bother Albert. His hands were bare now, and Albert could study his uncle's fingers—long and slender, but strangely squared-off at the ends. The backs of his hands were covered with silky blond hair that reminded Albert of spider filament caught in slanting light. "Your grandmother doesn't approve of actresses." He leaned close to whisper again. "Do you know your mother tried to become an actress herself?"

"Well—" Albert began, not knowing exactly what to say. He wanted to tell Uncle Clay that Mother wasn't as silly as Zora LaRue; that if Mother ever became an actress, she wouldn't end up believing in things like divorce. But he didn't have to say anything. Up the aisle, Virginia and Mother were returning to their seats at last.

Albert turned to look out the window, feeling disloyal. So that was why Uncle Claybourne had suddenly come to London. He and Grandmother Trask had read about Zora LaRue in the newspaper and were worried that Mother might start getting dangerous opinions like hers.

Even though Albert agreed with some of the things Uncle Clay had said about Miss LaRue, he wasn't sure that all actresses were bad. He tried to remember exactly what he'd said to his uncle. Had he let Mother down? He hadn't meant to. Father would be disappointed in him if he'd done that.

The excitement he'd felt earlier about going home slowly strung apart and faded, like paint from a watercolor brush dipped into a tumbler of water.

Three

Wednesday, April 10, 1912.   9:20 A.M.

So that was the *Titanic*!

With so many dockside structures and smaller vessels blocking his view, Albert couldn't see the entire outline of the ship from the train window. But he saw enough to appreciate the liner's size. Her enormous mass overshadowed the shipping offices, and her row of funnels looked like four stubs of broomstick rammed into an oval wedding cake.

From his reading Albert knew all about the *Titanic*. Her nine decks made her as high as an eleven-story building. And she was 882 feet long, almost equal to four city blocks. If stood on end she would be taller than any skyscraper in the world—even taller than the lofty Washington Monument, which dwarfed all the buildings in Albert's own city and had always seemed to him like the finger of God pointing toward heaven.

Excitement burned again in Albert's stomach.

While Mother in her plumed hat, leather gloves, and silky fur stole sat nervously on the edge of her seat, and Virginia swung the twins-in-a-cradle plaything that Mother had folded from a handkerchief, the train shuffled through Terminus Station, crossed Southampton's Canute Road, and lumbered to a stop beside the platform running parallel to the quay.

"Southampton dock!" called the conductor, and hordes of people swarmed up the aisles, through the open doors, and down the thumping metal steps.

The wind blew briskly. Above the murmurs of the crowd, Albert could hear flags and pennants whipping on their poles. Most dockside buildings and ships in port flew at least one ensign. The *Titanic* displayed two. A blue flag waved from the liner's stern, and a red pennant with a white star flapped from her mainmast. The star was the symbol of the White Star line, a luxury steamship company operating out of Britain. But Albert knew the real owner was J. P. Morgan, an American millionaire even richer than Colonel John Jacob Astor, who the newspapers reported would be sailing on the *Titanic* today.

As porters unloaded luggage from the train and set it on huge trolleys, Uncle Clay approached a man in a blue uniform. "Where do second-class passengers board?"

Mother shivered slightly, but Albert seemed to be the only one who noticed.

The man pointed with an elbow. "Gangway aft. That way. No hurry, though, if you'd like to see the town. She doesn't sail till noon."

Uncle Claybourne turned to Mother. "Would you care to walk around the town?"

Holding Virginia's hand, Mother addressed Albert. "Tell your uncle, 'No thank you.'"

Albert ignored the request, but Virginia transmitted the message for him. "Mum says, 'No thank you,'" she piped.

Uncle Clay looked icily at Mother, but she pretended not to notice. He jerked his head stiffly. "Very well. Come on." He started off briskly in the direction the officer had pointed, Mother and Albert following more slowly with Virginia.

OOO-EEE-OOM! Suddenly the ship's siren blared. Birds fled. Windowpanes clattered.

Virginia jumped. "What was that?"

One of the porters pushing a nearby trolley stopped to answer. "Breaks your eardrums, that whistle. And it's been blasting all morning. Telling people the *Titanic* will sail today. Well, I, for one, would believe it without all that noise."

"Mum and Albert and I are going to America on the *Titanic*," Virginia offered.

"That right?"

"But Mum and I don't want to."

"Well, well. And why not?"

"We want—"

Mother pulled on Virginia's hand. "Come along, dear." The three of them hurried until Uncle Clay was only a few feet ahead of them. Passengers were boarding the ship on several gangways both fore and aft, but Uncle Claybourne walked past a gangway marked *Third Class* and headed for another.

Virginia studied a sign they passed. "*R.M.S. Titanic*," she read.

For once Mother smiled. "Why, that's wonderful, dear. Did Miss Harcher teach you to read *Titanic*?"

"Mm-hmm. And she taught me what R.M.S. means: Royal Mail Steamer. That's because the *Titanic* carries letters all the way across the ocean."

"Very good," said Mother. "I'm proud of you. Miss Harcher did a fine job teaching you your letters."

"So why can't we take her to Washington?"

Mother's smile dissolved. "Hurry up. Uncle Claybourne has our tickets. We have to stay with him."

Albert heard the squeak of pulleys as huge electric cranes hoisted steamer trunks and boxes to the upper decks. There seemed to be hundreds of porters and crewmen scurrying about to get the quantities of luggage and milling passengers on board.

Ahead, Uncle Clay had paused to wait for the rest of the family. "This way. This is our entrance."

All four Trasks joined the throng of second-class passengers funneling up the long, steep gangway to the C Deck entrance of the ship.

The officer who greeted them smiled warmly, then checked Uncle Claybourne's tickets against the passenger list. "You'll be in cabins D 66 and D 68. That's one deck below, by the second-class dining saloon. The stairs and lift are straight on."

"A lift?" cried Virginia. "Just like Harrods!"

"Won't that be splendid?" said Albert, trying to cheer the grown-ups. "An elevator in second class. We didn't have an elevator in first class coming over."

But Mother didn't speak as they walked in the direction the officer had pointed. Not in the hallway with thick red carpeting. Not in the wood-paneled elevator. Not even to the youthful cabin steward who met them in the hallway and told them his life story as he unlocked their rooms.

"I'm George Sloan from Southampton. You can call me Georgie. With the coal strike what's been going on, crews on all the ships has been out of work since January. But me and Papa turned out last week for the *Titanic* hiring and both of us was signed on. Bit of luck, what? Me papa's a restaurant steward in first class. Me mum's home with four little ones, so she'll be glad to see those wages coming in again. I've been a page on White Star ships for three years, but this was the first time they'd take me as cabin steward. That's 'cause I'm growed up now. Seventeen."

Georgie turned, bright-eyed, to Uncle Claybourne. "Well, I expect this is the cabin you and the missus will be wanting. It's got that elegant double bed. Gen-u-wine brass, it is. The other room has two bunks, such as the crew sleeps in."

Uncle Clay put one gloved hand to his mouth and coughed nervously. "Uh—Mrs. Trask is my sister-in-law. I'll be sharing a room with my nephew. He and I will take the other room if it's all right with him."

Albert nodded.

"Sorry," said Georgie. "No offense. I saw *Mr. C. Trask and Mrs. K. Trask* on the passenger list and naturally expected you was man and wife."

Mother glared. This conversation wasn't improving her mood. "Will the trunks be here soon?"

"Yes, missus. I expect they will. The porters are working fast as greased magic to get everything aboard. Won't be long now. A button will be bringing your things to your cabins right soon."

"Button?" repeated Virginia.

"Bellboy," explained Georgie. "*Buttons* is what we calls the lads."

Albert smiled to himself. At seventeen Georgie was probably younger than lots of the bellmen, but he obviously felt superior.

"Is there anything else I can get you now?" Georgie asked.

Virginia was trying to reach the faucet of one of the two marble-topped sinks. "Does this water turn on?"

"Yes, miss. It sure does. Hot and cold twenty-four hours a day." Georgie showed her how to work the faucet and how to empty the water afterward by lifting the basin up. Then he showed Mother how to work the space heater near the bed. "It's a right elegant room, it is."

Georgie seemed to be waiting for Mother's response, but she didn't offer it.

"Yes, it's newer and a lot bigger than the cabin we came to England in," said Albert.

"We came in first class," said Virginia.

Mother stared at the light fixture, saying nothing.

"Well, I'll be seeing to me other passengers, then. If you need me, just ring that bell." Georgie pointed to an electric bell on the wall. "Oh, I almost forgot. I'm obliged—White Star company rules—to show you the life belts. Nothing's going to happen what's you'll need them, of course, but I have to show you anyways." He opened the closet door and pulled out two large white vests.

"That's silly," said Virginia. "Albert says the *Titanic* can't sink. He's read all about it."

Georgie winked at Mother. "Wide awake little ones

you've got there. Smart as whips. I've got me a sister and brother what's just like 'em."

Mother stitched her lips together, nodding slightly.

Georgie headed for the door. "Well, ta-ta, then."

"Thank you for your help. We'll be seeing you," said Uncle Claybourne. As the steward closed the door, Uncle Clay looked from the built-in sofa covered with tapestry to the cushioned wicker chair. He was probably waiting for Mother's invitation to sit down. But she stood rigid as a flagpole, the lavender plume on her wide hat floating like an ensign carried into battle. "Well, Albert," said his uncle. "Shall we go to our own cabin?"

Before Albert could answer, Virginia plopped down on the sofa. "Oh, Mum, you and I could sleep on the bed, and Miss Harcher could sleep here. *Why* can't we take Miss Harcher?"

Uncle Claybourne scowled. "Because we can't, that's why. And I don't want to hear that question ever again. Do you hear me?"

Virginia sprang to her feet. Mother slammed her purse and satchel on the bed and charged over to Uncle Clay, the lavender plume on her hat bobbing up and down. "I told you not to interfere with my children. You're not their father. You may not discipline them."

"Oh, for heaven's sake, Katherine," said Uncle Clay. "Stop yelling like a fishwife. People can hear you all over this ship."

"Oh, they can, can they? Well, that's no business of yours, Claybourne Trask. You and your mother may be able to control where I live, but you can't control how I think or talk."

Snuffling noises were coming from the side of the room, and Albert looked over to see Virginia throw herself down on the sofa again. "Ooh! My stomach hurts!" she wailed. "I have 'pendicitis."

Talk about actresses, Albert thought. Ginny could teach that Zora LaRue a thing or two.

Mother rushed over to Virginia and stroked her head. "Oh, darling, where does your stomach hurt?"

Virginia clutched her stomach. "Here. It hurts bad," she sobbed.

Uncle Claybourne spoke aside to Albert. "Does she have appendicitis?"

"Only when she doesn't get her own way. She knows appendicitis is what killed Father and that Mother goes crazy when she hears the word. But Ginny doesn't even know which side of her stomach her appendix is on. Look at her. She's holding the left side."

Virginia moved her hand. "It hurts here too."

"Dr. Mendenhall said the pain can start on the left side sometimes," Mother reported.

Albert rolled his eyes toward Uncle Clay. "Mother took her to Dr. Mendenhall three times in London. He said Ginny doesn't have appendicitis."

Mother's nostrils flared. "He said he wasn't certain. Appendicitis is very hard to diagnose. Your father died because his doctor in Washington didn't diagnose it in time."

"I need Miss Harcher!" wailed Virginia. "Miss Harcher has medicine that makes my 'pendicitis better."

"Sugar water," Albert muttered to no one in particular.

Mother pulled Ginny to a sitting position. "Help me,

Clay," she cried. "We need to get her off the ship. We need to find a doctor right now."

"Now, now, Kitty. Don't panic. I'm sure there's an infirmary on shipboard."

"A hospital," Albert confirmed. "It's on this level. We passed it when we got off the elevator."

"They can't operate on a ship," Mother cried. "What if she needs surgery?"

"Calm down, Kitty. It doesn't help Virginia to see you lose control. And it's very likely the hospital is equipped to operate."

"Don't just stand there!" Mother ordered. "Ring for Georgie! See if he can get us a wheelchair so she won't have to walk!"

Albert rolled his eyes at the ceiling.

Four

—————————— ✑ ——————————

Wednesday, April 10, 1912.   11:55 A.M.

OOO-EEE-OOM! OOO-EEE-OOM!

The *Titanic*'s whistles seemed louder than before, more urgent. On the stern, or aft end of the boat deck, which was reserved for second-class passengers, Albert stood near the railing to witness the departure of the *Titanic* from the dock in Southampton.

Standing on the bow would have been more fun, but the forward part of the deck was reserved for first-class passengers. Between the first- and second-class areas was the large officers' portion of the deck with barriers on either side to keep passengers where they belonged.

Albert hated being alone when everyone else up here seemed to have someone to share the excitement with. But Mother and Uncle Claybourne had taken Virginia to the hospital in the wheelchair Georgie had provided. Well, at least Mother and Uncle Clay were speaking to each other again, Albert told himself. And at least Mother had suggested Albert watch the departure by himself.

The earlier wind gusts had eased to a less-chilling breeze, and for England the weather was pleasant—sunny and around fifty degrees. People were pushing toward the best lookout spots, waiting for the ship to set sail. Along the railing of this open deck, throngs of passengers had crowded to signal their good-byes to the hundreds of well-wishers far below on the quay.

He studied the scene from every angle, etching the details into his memory to record later in the art tablet he'd foolishly neglected to bring with him. At the same time, for no reason, he reached inside his pocket to stroke the familiar metal of Father's watch.

An old man standing next to Albert patted his arm. "Look, that man up there is waving to us!"

Sure enough. On the *Oceanic*, which was docked some distance away, a man had climbed to the high lookout post and was waving with wide sweeps of his arm. Albert pulled off his cap to wave back.

As he did so, Albert noticed other well-wishers on the *Oceanic*'s many decks, scores of them waving and shouting with voices too far away to be understood. According to Georgie, who had delivered another monologue when he brought Virginia's wheelchair, the British ship *Oceanic* and the American ship *New York*, which were moored together in Southampton harbor, would remain in port for a while. Coal was still in short supply after the three-month miners' strike, and the *Titanic* would need all that was available for her maiden crossing to America.

Voices and laughter carried over the deck. Somewhere a harmonica was playing "Alexander's Ragtime Band."

Then suddenly Albert heard a new noise—a mechanical one—and felt a vibration through the ship's hull. The great engines turned over. Steam flowed thickly high above his head through the ship's first three funnels. The "Floating Palace" Albert had read so much about was off, and dozens of men and boys ran along the quay, trying to keep pace. The *Titanic* moved regally along the dock toward the anchored *Oceanic* and *New York*.

All at once six shots blasted, like reports from a rifle. Six ropes, thick as elephant trunks, soared high in the air before falling back into the terrified crowd on the quay.

"The *New York* is loose!" yelled the man standing next to Albert. "Her moorings snapped."

"Suction!" said another man. "We've created suction! There's not room in this port for a ship as big as ours to move."

"The *New York*'s coming straight at us!" screamed a woman.

Passengers elbowed and shoved each other, scrambling for safety. As if drawn by magnetic force, the *New York* was drifting backward toward the stern of the *Titanic*, directly toward the spot where Albert had been standing. Both ships seemed doomed.

If the ships were in trouble, Albert was at least near the lifeboats, he realized. But more than ever he wished his family had come here with him.

On the *New York*'s deck, sailors were running back and forth, draping huge mats across the boat deck railing to soften the collision.

On the *Titanic* Albert heard seamen shouting to each other. Suddenly the *Titanic*'s engines died, and the suction ended. With only feet to spare, the *New York* turned, drifting another way.

An old gentleman leaning on his cane crossed himself.

A baby started to cry. "That's all right, dear," soothed the mother. "It's all over now."

Other sighs of relief were drowned by loud music.

Albert spun around to see a man in a blue uniform who was marching around the deck and playing "The Roast Beef of Old England" on his bugle.

"Well, I guess that means it's lunchtime," a woman in a blue hat said to her friend. "Shall we go to the dining saloon?"

"Lunchtime!" exclaimed her friend. "You won't catch me eating on this ship."

"You'll have a long fast, then. We won't be in New York until next week."

"Listen to me, Lilly Dastrup," said the woman's friend. "I'm the daughter of a sailor and the sister of a sailor, and sailors' families have an instinct for calamities at sea. I knew I shouldn't have let you talk me into coming on this ship, and what we just witnessed proves it. The *Titanic* will never reach New York City."

"*Tsh*," said Lilly.

"Don't *tsh* me. Doesn't the name of the ship we nearly rammed into tell you anything?"

"Oh, Dora, you're not going to repeat all those old sailing superstitions again!"

"Make fun of me if you like, but I know what I know," Dora sniffed. "If a ship doesn't leave port well, she won't reach port well. I never did trust this fancy *Titanic* anyway. I told you about that prophecy I read."

"You mean that novel you keep talking about?"

"Yes, *Futility* by Mr. Morgan Robertson. I read it fourteen years ago, but I'm a sailor's daughter, and I'll remember that book till the day I die. It's all about a ship named the *Titan* that's exactly like this *Titanic* we're standing on right here, and just as big and sinful. She set sail in April, just like we're doing, and she sank in the ice fields in the middle of the Atlantic. She didn't have enough lifeboats to rescue people, and most everyone was lost. You mark my words. That was prophecy pure and simple."

Albert strained to hear more.

"But the *Titanic* doesn't need lifeboats," Lilly reasoned. "She's unsinkable. Everyone knows that."

"Hmmph. That's exactly what the people in the book said about the *Titan*. I tell you, sailors' families have an instinct for these things. I'm going to get off this terrible ship at Cherbourg when she docks in France early this evening. And if you have any sense, you'll come with me."

The women wandered off, and Albert heard no more of their conversation. He wasn't superstitious, of course, and didn't believe in all those old-fashioned sailors' warnings about evil omens and prophecy. But it would be interesting to learn about the *Titanic*'s lifeboats. He'd try to remember to count them sometime when he didn't have anything better to do.

Right now he had something else to worry about. Virginia. She didn't really have appendicitis, did she? he wondered. Wasn't she just faking again?

For no reason, Albert had a queasy feeling inside.

Five

Virginia certainly didn't act very sick to Albert. In fact, he'd been studying her for a whole day now, and she seemed just fine.

He watched as his sister hopped up from the wooden deck of the C Promenade where she'd been sitting cross-legged with her new friend, Sarah Brewer. Virginia climbed back into her wheelchair. "I'm the queen and this is my throne," she said to Sarah. "You're my lady-in-waiting."

"What's that?" Sarah asked.

Ginny had made friends with the Brewer family—a mother and three children who had sat at the dining table with Albert and Uncle Clay for last night's dinner and again this morning for breakfast. The Brewers were re-turning to America after three years in Ceylon, where they'd been missionaries, and six-year-old Sarah apparently wasn't as interested in queens as Virginia was.

"A lady-in-waiting is a person who does what the queen says," Ginny explained. "Tuck my blanket in."

"Huh?"

"Tuck my blanket around me. Tight."

"All right." Sarah did as she was ordered.

"You didn't cover my feet. They'll get cold."

Albert looked over at Mother to see if she was reassured to know that Ginny was no longer dying, but Mother had fallen asleep. Wrapped in a wool blanket on her deck chair, she looked like a larva in a cocoon.

Poor Mother. This was the first time she'd slept in twenty-four hours, and she hadn't gone to the dining saloon in all that time either. The doctor who had examined Virginia yesterday didn't think she had appendicitis, but he was concerned about her family history and Ginny's personal history of stomachaches, so he'd kept her overnight in the hospital for observation. It turned out, though, that he hadn't found time to do much observing himself. Mother had done most of it, staying awake all night at Ginny's bedside.

So far, this sailing wasn't turning out at all like the family excursion Albert had looked forward to. If Father were here—if he were still alive—things would be different, Albert told himself. Mother would be cheerful and relaxed. Virginia wouldn't be able to upset everyone by throwing tantrums. The family would do everything on the ship together: Watch the offshore loading of passengers and provisions yesterday at Cherbourg, France. Dine on poached halibut in dill sauce last night in the elegant oak-paneled dining saloon. Walk under the stars around the open upper deck as the chamber orchestra far away in the first-class lounge played selections from *The Tales of Hoffman* and *Cavalleria Rusticana*.

But Father wasn't here, and Albert had done all of those things alone. Mother had been so worried about Virginia's so-called stomachache that she'd refused to leave Ginny's side. And bachelors like Uncle Clay didn't understand the importance of families. After dinner last night he'd gone to the men's smoking room to play bridge with three companions. And instead of staying with his family on the C Deck Promenade this morning, he was playing cards again right now.

"Now get me my crown," Virginia told her lady-in-waiting.

"You don't have one."

"This is pretend, silly. Get me a pretend crown."

"All right," said Sarah.

"You don't say 'All right' to the queen. You curtsy and say, 'Yes, your majesty.'"

Sarah bowed awkwardly. "Yes, your majesty." She walked over to her empty deck chair by the ones where the other members of her family were sitting and picked up an invisible crown.

Noticing Sarah's older sister, Emily, Albert frowned slightly. He didn't care as much for the Brewers as Virginia did. Sarah was the liveliest of the bunch and the same age as Virginia, so he could understand the attraction there. But two-year-old Robert was pale and sickly and seldom left the lap of his stern-faced mother, who wore plain black dresses with a cameo at her neck and piled her hair on her head in a tight, old-fashioned way.

And twelve-year-old Emily. Well! She was a definite

pain. Oh, Albert had to admit she was pretty enough, with a turned-up nose and strawberry blond hair that she pulled back at her neck and tied with a bow even bigger than the one on top of Virginia's head. But she was a year younger than Albert, and she treated him as if he didn't have a brain in his head. Last night at dinner, when Uncle Clay had asked him how his Latin lessons were going, Emily had taken it upon herself to recite (with practically no encouragement from anyone else) a poem from the *Tristia* by Ovid. And right now she was reading something called *Lives of the Saints and Martyrs*. Albert doubted if even Miss Harcher—as dull and ridiculous as that woman was—would read such a dopey-sounding book.

Sarah returned to Virginia's wheelchair. "Here's your crown, queen."

"Well, put it on my head."

Emily looked up from her book, and for an instant her eyes met Albert's before he quickly turned away. He certainly didn't want that stupid girl to think he'd been looking at her.

"I'm hungry," Queen Virginia told her lady-in-waiting. "Get me some tea and scones."

The mention of food reminded Albert that he was hungry too. Wasn't it about time the bugler came by to announce luncheon? He took Father's watch from his pocket and opened the cover: 11:34. What wonderful menu would the dining stewards be serving for lunch today?

"I want to be the queen now," Sarah said.

"Not yet," said Virginia. "It's still my turn."

Sarah made a face. "I'm tired of being lady-in-waiting," she whined.

Emily looked up from her book again, this time at the younger girls. "Would you like me to read you a story?"

"Yes, yes," said Sarah. "Read us about the martyrs."

Albert rolled his eyes. Six-year-old Sarah wanted to learn about the martyrs? The entire Brewer family was crazy, he decided. Completely dotty.

Emily moved to another deck chair to make room for Virginia and Sarah on either side of her. Ginny scrambled out of her wheelchair and climbed into a chair beside Emily.

Mother rolled over in her sleep.

Where was the bugler? Albert wondered again. He hoped the luncheon menu would be as splendid as last night's halibut.

With a sigh Albert stood up and looked out the window. The sea was calm. In the distance he could see gray mountains slowly rising out of the ocean like a family of whales surfacing for air. They were at Queenstown!

He rushed over to Mother and touched her gently on the arm. "Wake up, Mother. We're approaching land. Come see Ireland."

The deck chair squeaked as Mother turned away.

He sat on the edge of her chair. "Don't you want to see Ireland?"

"Mmm. Not now."

"Oh, come on. You'll be sorry if you don't look. We may never come back here again." Straining, he pulled her partway up.

Mother sighed. "Very well." She stood listlessly, allowing him to walk her slowly across the deck.

In the few minutes he'd been gone from the window,

the scene had changed. The ship was closer to land now, and the dazzling morning sun had emerged from a cloud to turn the Irish hillsides green as peppermint leaves. Here and there, Albert could make out groups of dwellings above the shoreline cliffs. "Isn't it splendid?"

Mother yawned. "Beautiful."

"Your grandmother came from Ireland, didn't she?"

"Yes."

"You told me you always wanted to go there."

"Yes. Your father promised to take me there so I could see the people make lace. He was going to buy me a lace tablecloth. I always wanted one just like my grandmother's."

Albert had an idea. "Let's buy one. We can get off the ship at Queenstown. I'm sure the officers will let us. A few people got off last night at Cherbourg. I'll go ask someone if we can."

Mother looked anxiously toward Virginia. "No. The doctor said Ginny shouldn't walk too far."

"I'll push her in the wheelchair."

Mother shook her head. "No. She needs to stay near the hospital on the ship, in case of an emergency."

Emergency? Not unless they asked little Sarah Bernhardt to do something she wasn't in the mood for. But Albert didn't say what he was thinking. "She's feeling lots better now. I've been watching her. She's been jumping up and down."

Mother smiled. "Really?"

"Let's get off the ship and go to Queenstown," he urged her.

All at once Albert heard the merry strains of "The Roast Beef of Old England" and saw the bugler approaching. He wanted to see Ireland, but he hated to miss one of the fancy meals on the *Titanic*. He felt torn.

Mother settled the issue. "We can't leave the ship now. Let's put Ginny in her wheelchair and go to the dining saloon. I'm starved."

Albert shrugged and followed Mother to the other side of the deck.

"Are you hungry, darling?" Mother asked Virginia.

"Yes. I want some tea and scones."

"They don't serve tea and scones at lunch," said Emily. "They're serving haddock almondine. I saw the menu."

Haddock almondine? Albert's mouth watered.

"What's haddock ah-ding?" Virginia asked.

"It's wonderful," Albert said.

"It has nuts on it," Mother added. "You love nuts."

"What is it?" Virginia demanded.

"Fish," said Emily.

Why didn't that smart aleck mind her own business? Albert thought. Ginny hated fish.

"I want tea and scones," Virginia repeated.

"The dining saloon isn't a restaurant where you can order what you want," Albert said. "You have to eat what they serve."

Virginia turned to Mother. "They brought tea and scones to the hospital for us. Tell them to bring some out here."

"Mother and I want haddock almondine," Albert said. "Get in your wheelchair, and I'll push you to the dining saloon."

"Ooh!" Virginia doubled over, clutching her stomach. "I have 'pendicitis! The doctor said people with 'pendicitis don't have to eat anything they don't want."

"Get in your wheelchair," Albert ordered.

Mother put her hand on his shoulder. "No, no, Albert. I'll stay out here with her. Tell the dining steward to send us some tea and scones."

"You need to eat, Mother. You should go to the dining saloon."

"No, Ginny's right," Mother said. "The doctor said not to force her to eat. And tea will soothe her stomach. I'll stay here with her."

"No, I'll stay with her," Albert said. "You haven't eaten since we left London. I'm not hungry," he lied.

"She may need me. What if there's an emergency?"

Albert sighed. "I'll come get you if she needs you."

"Well—" said Mother. "I *am* hungry."

Six

Virginia licked strawberry jam from her fingers and grinned with satisfaction. She had wolfed down both her scones and one of Albert's too.

He eyed the crumbs on the tea cart, wishing the steward had brought six scones instead of only four. He thought of the lucky people in the dining saloon eating as much as they wanted. He thought of the white linen cloths on the tables and the stewards in their spotless uniforms. He thought of the oak-paneled walls and the richly carved pedestal chairs and the blue and white bone china without a single mar or chip. Mostly he thought of haddock almondine. Mouthwatering haddock almondine. Compared to the elegant meals on the *Titanic*, even Mattie Lou's cooking at Grandmother's house—even her peanut soup served with hot biscuits and honey—seemed countrified and boring.

Virginia belched loudly.

Pig, Albert thought.

"Emily Brewer loves you," Virginia suddenly blurted.

"Huh?"

"Emily loves you."

Albert's cheeks grew warm. "That's stupid. She doesn't even know me."

Ginny shrugged. "She loves you anyway."

"Who said?"

"She did. She said you looked handsome in your long trousers last night."

Without thinking, Albert reached for the pocket of his houndstooth jacket. He'd managed to pin it from the inside with three safety pins, but he hadn't been able to make it lie flat, and the pins showed through slightly. Mother had been so upset yesterday he hadn't dared tell her the jacket was torn. Now, dressed in knickers again, he felt like a child, especially with a pocket that was pinned in place.

"Well, I don't love Emily."

"Yes, you do. You're always looking at her."

"I am not!"

"You were looking at her the whole time Sarah and I were playing 'queen.' "

"Liar!"

"Don't you want to know what else she said?"

Albert considered his answer to that question. Of course he wanted to know what Emily had said about him. But he didn't want Ginny to think he did. "Not especially."

"She said you remind her of her papa," Virginia reported. "She misses her papa."

Well. What was that supposed to mean?

Virginia reached for her plate on the tea cart and held it up to her face so she could lick the remains of strawberry jam.

Albert cringed. How could his sister be so disgusting?

As she set the plate back on the cart, she thought of something else she wanted. "Let me hold your watch."

"No. Your hands are dirty."

She wiped them on the sides of her dress. "There. Give it to me."

Frowning, Albert took a napkin from the cart and dipped a corner into the cooling pot of water they'd used for their tea. "Here. Wipe your hands with this. Your face too."

Ginny did as she was told, then reached for the watch again. "Give it to me."

"Oh, all right." Albert bent close to her so the chain would reach far enough and removed Father's watch from his pocket. "There."

"I want to look at it in my lap. Unhook the chain."

"You'll drop it and break it."

"I will not."

"You always say you won't break things, but then you do anyway."

"Emily lets Sarah hold her books."

"So?"

"Both of them," Ginny added. "The one about the saints and martyrs. And the one with the poems by the dead man who used to live in Rome."

Bully for Emily, Albert thought. Maybe she'll grow up to read stories about saints and martyrs to every pitiful child she ever meets. Maybe she'll spend her entire life on ships and trains, torturing adults in every country of the world by reciting Ovid.

"What does that have to do with anything?" he asked.

"Their papa gave Emily those books before he died. She always reads them, the way you always look at Papa's watch."

Albert drew in his breath. That wasn't quite the explanation he'd expected.

"Unhook your watch," Virginia repeated. "I want to hold it."

No, Albert wanted to say.

"He was my father too," Ginny added.

"Well—" said Albert, releasing the fob. He was unable to argue with Ginny's logic. "Be careful."

She took it clumsily, sprung open the cover, then shut it again with a click.

What was it about Albert that reminded Emily of her father? He wanted to ask Virginia straight out but decided not to show too much interest. Instead, he thought of a less direct question as he studied his hands in his lap. "How did their father die?"

Virginia opened and shut the watch cover. "Sarah said her papa got some strange sickness in the place where he was a missionary. The doctors in Cey-Cey—Ceylon didn't have any medicine for it."

Albert felt a pang in his chest. He wondered how old Mr. Brewer had been. Older than Father? Father had died at thirty-six. Only thirty-six! Albert remembered how unfair that had seemed, how deserted he'd felt. How angry. He hadn't been able to sleep or do his lessons or even finish his sketches of the White House.

Then one day, when Mother had left Virginia with a

friend while she went to the cemetery, Albert had walked by himself to Rock Creek Park. And there, in a secluded spot, away from the picnickers and hikers and botany students, he'd picked up a stick and hit the ground with it as hard as he could, yelling and yelling, louder than the lions or elephants in their cages, until he wore out every bit of his strength.

His throat hurt when he got home, and his arm was tired, but he felt lots better inside.

Ginny's small voice brought Albert back to the present. "Robert has the sickness too. Robert will probably die."

Albert looked up, shocked. Robert was only two. And Virginia shouldn't talk so casually about death. "Who said?" he raged.

Ginny shrugged. "Everybody, I guess." As she spoke, she went on clicking the watch cover open and shut. "They're taking Robert home to see if the doctors in America have any medicine for his sickness. But I told them to go to London. He needs Miss Harcher's medicine."

"He does not! And stop playing with Father's watch that way! It isn't a toy!"

"I didn't say it was a toy." Click. Click. Click.

"*Stop playing with it!*"

Albert reached for the watch, but Virginia clung tightly.

"It's my turn," she said. "You've had it ever since Papa died."

He tried to pry her fingers from the chain. "Give it to me!"

"No. If you don't let me keep it, I'll—I'll—"

"You'll what?"

"I'll tell Emily you love her."

Albert's voice was low, husky. "You do and I'll smack your face."

"Oh, keep your old watch!" She hurled it as hard as she could, and Albert heard it strike twice—on a deck chair, on the wooden floor.

He rushed over, picked up the watch, and held it to his ear. Miraculously, it was still ticking, but the cover was bent so badly that the clasp wouldn't shut. Quivering, he stared at it. Could it be fixed? Where could he take it?

At last he stuffed it in his pocket, ran back to the wheelchair where his sister was still sitting, and grabbed her by the shoulders. He wanted to shake some sense into her. "You broke it!" he yelled. "You threw it on purpose!"

"*Oow!* You're hurting me!"

He was glad if she hurt. He wanted to shake her until she begged for mercy. "You're a brat. A little—" Suddenly he remembered the word Uncle Clay had used, the word Albert had looked up in the *Titanic*'s library. "You're obstreperous!"

"I am not! Mummy!" she cried. "Mummy!"

From nowhere Mother appeared and seized his arm. "Albert! What are you doing to your little sister?"

"Mummy!" Now that Mother was here, now that the little actress had her audience, Virginia burst into tears. She rubbed her shoulder. "He hurt me! He called me a bad name! He said he was going to smack my face!"

"Albert Trask! You didn't!"

"He called me ob-ob-ob—a brat," Ginny added between sobs.

Albert didn't believe in tattling, but Virginia's crime was unpardonable. "She broke Father's watch."

"I—didn't—mean—to," Virginia sobbed.

Mother bent to hug her. "Of course you didn't." She turned angrily to Albert. "She's just a baby! When will you understand that?"

Baby! She was six years old, for heaven's sake.

"My stomach hurts," Virginia wailed. "I have 'pendicitis."

Mother looked stricken. "Oh, darling. Does it still hurt? I'll wheel you back to the hospital and have the doctor take another look at you."

There were a hundred things Albert wanted to say, a hundred things he wanted to yell, but he didn't. He wouldn't stoop to Virginia's level. Instead, he grabbed for the wheelchair. "I'll push her."

"Don't bother," Mother said sarcastically, prying Albert's hands away. "If you can't be trusted alone with your sister long enough for me to eat lunch, she certainly doesn't need you now."

Seven

Thursday, April 11, 1912.   12:45 P.M.

At the railing Albert studied Father's watch, his stomach rocking like the ocean. Virginia deserved far worse punishment than he'd given her. When Albert was six, he'd certainly known better than to throw a pocket watch, especially not the one Mother had given Father on their wedding day. He studied it, touching the dent in the cover.

"Hello," said a high, clear voice. Emily Brewer's.

She'd never spoken to him before except to recite Latin poetry. Albert was in no mood for that. He didn't answer. Maybe she'd get the hint and leave.

"You missed a wonderful lunch," Emily said.

Tell it to Virginia, Albert thought.

"Haddock almondine," Emily said. "The best I've ever tasted."

Why didn't she just shut up? Why didn't she go away?

"I've never tasted meals like the ones they serve on this ship," Emily continued. "Have you?"

"Of course," Albert lied. "My grandmother's cook in McLean knows lots better recipes than the chefs on this ship." He stared at the ocean.

"I found out what that boat's all about," Emily said.

Albert didn't answer.

"Don't you want to know about the boat?"

Albert spoke through tight lips. "What boat?"

She pointed down, near the hull of the ship. "That one."

Albert didn't look. He didn't need to. "It's one of the tenders that brought the mail and Irish passengers to the ship."

"No, it isn't. It's a new boat. The two tenders are still there. Don't you ever pay attention to anything?"

Albert wanted to punch her. He'd do it too, if she were a boy. Casually he looked down.

"Well," she said, "aren't you going to ask me?"

Albert hesitated.

"It's waiting for the lace merchants," she blurted. "Irish lace merchants. They rented the boat in Queenstown so they could come sell lace to the rich people in the *Titanic*'s first class. And you'll never believe this. Some rich man named Astor just bought his wife a lace bed jacket that cost eight hundred dollars in American money. Imagine! He spent eight hundred dollars for something that no one will ever see but the two of them! That's more than my parents used to earn in a year. Maybe your father earned more than that, when he was alive, but it's still a lot of money."

Albert wondered if Emily expected him to say something about the fact that her papa was dead too, but he didn't care to.

"Your father was a lawyer," Emily said. "I guess he left your family better fixed than Papa left us."

Mother's annuity was none of Emily's business—even if Albert had time to discuss it right now, which he didn't. But Emily had given him an idea about how to make peace with Mother for shaking his sister. "Are they selling anything besides bed jackets? Any other kind of lace?"

"Well, I certainly hope so. Not many people in this world are willing to waste perfectly good money on anything as silly as a bed jacket."

"I've got to go," Albert explained. "There's something I have to do."

He took off before she had time to answer, the soles of his high-top brown oxfords clopping on the wooden deck and then thumping on the red-carpeted stairs as he bounded them, two at a time, to the gentlemen's smoking room one flight up on B Deck. Panting, he flung open the heavy door and looked around the spacious room, which was thick with the suffocating odor of pipe tobacco and cigars.

At the moment the room was less than one-third full, and Albert easily spotted his uncle sitting with three friends. He ran over.

"Forgive me, sir. I'm sorry to bother you, sir, but this is an emergency."

Uncle Claybourne looked up from his green leather armchair. He seemed doubtful. "Well, all right, Albert. I'm the dummy for this hand. Gentlemen, would you excuse me a moment while I speak to my nephew?"

As the others nodded and mumbled, Uncle Clay rose

and led Albert to a red leather settee in a secluded part of the room. "Yes? What's the trouble?"

Albert took a deep breath. "I need to borrow some money."

Uncle Clay reached for his black billfold and started to open it. "Well, I'm sure it's important or you wouldn't ask. How much do you need?"

Albert had considered that question on the way up the stairs. Mrs. Astor's bed jacket cost eight hundred dollars, but it was probably made of the finest lace you could buy. Great-grandmother Kelly had been married to a farmer, so she wouldn't own anything that nice. "I—I'm not sure. Two hundred dollars should do it, I think."

"Two hundred dollars!" Uncle Clay closed the billfold.

Albert talked rapidly, realizing there was little time. "I have nearly thirty dollars hidden in our cabin. But I was hoping you could let me work the rest of it off when we get to Washington. I'd come to your office after school every day. Sweep. Wash windows. Things like that. I'd even come to your house and help your maid make beds and wash the dishes if you wanted me to."

"A hundred and seventy dollars is a lot of money, Albert. It would take you a long time to work that off. You're not in trouble, are you? You haven't broken something or stolen—"

"Oh, no, sir. Nothing like that. It's for Mother. She's always wanted an Irish lace tablecloth like her grandmother's, and there are lace merchants on the ship right now. They came over on a boat from Queenstown to sell their things to the ladies in first class."

"You'd borrow $170 to buy a tablecloth for your mother?"

Albert fidgeted with the flap on his torn pocket. "Well, she's worried about Ginny's stomachaches, and she's not very happy about—about this trip." He considered mentioning how Mother had caught him fighting with Virginia, but decided it was too personal. "She doesn't want to go back to Washington, you know."

His uncle nodded.

"I thought a lace tablecloth might cheer her up."

"Is that your only reason? At seventy-five cents a week, which is all I could pay you for what you're talking about, it would take nearly five years to pay off $170."

"Please, Uncle Clay. I promise to pay you back. And the merchants will leave the ship if we don't hurry."

Uncle Claybourne brushed his mustache with his fingers. "I don't like the idea of someone your age mortgaging the next five years of his life, Albert. But your mother does need cheering up right now, and I still have some money from your grandmother. How would it work if the two of you went in as partners? You give me your thirty dollars, and your grandmother can pay the rest."

"Oh, yes. Thank you, sir."

"Where's Katherine right now?"

"At the hospital. She took Ginny back there to see the doctor."

"We'll have to act fast. I'll find someone to take a message to one of the lace merchants, and you go get your mother."

"Uh—I think you should get Mother, Uncle Clay. She's not very happy with me right now."

Uncle Clay laughed out loud. It was the first time Albert could remember hearing his stone-faced uncle laugh like that, and the noise startled him. "So that's it, is it? She giving you the silent treatment? Well, let's hope a little Irish lace will warm her up for both of us. All right. You find a steward or page, and I'll get your mother. Run on now. I'll meet you on C Deck."

Eight

Thursday, April 11, 1912.   1:10 P.M.

As soon as Albert spoke to a page about getting a message to the lace merchants, he raced to C Deck to find Uncle Clay and Mother, but they hadn't arrived yet. No one was there except the Brewer family. Robert was sitting on Emily's lap while she read him a story.

Emily looked up briefly at Albert but pretended not to see him. She continued reading, her chirp-chirp of a voice peppering his ears like ammo from a peashooter:

Two of the Roman soldiers grabbed Sebastian by either arm, twisting them backward until he felt they would break.

"This Sebastian has pretended to be one of us, but he's a Christian in disguise."

"A Christian!" shouted another soldier. "Kill him!"

Then the soldiers tied him to a tree so he couldn't move and shot him with all their arrows.

Good night! Albert thought. Did Emily expect a two-year-old to listen to that kind of stuff? No wonder Robert was always sick.

Two seats away Sarah and Mrs. Brewer were huddled together.

"I'm the queen and you're my lady-in-waiting," Sarah told her mother. "That means you have to call me 'your majesty' and do everything I say."

"Yes, your majesty," said her mother. "Shall I serve you tea now on your gold dishes?"

Shaking his head, Albert walked to the window and looked down. The boat was still there, thank goodness. But would the page deliver the message to the merchants in time? He could see the tenders starting off toward the Irish shoreline, so the merchants' boat would probably be leaving soon. Why hadn't the tradesmen come yet? And where were Mother and Uncle Clay?

All at once he heard footsteps. He turned around to see two men and a woman rushing toward the Brewers. Smiling as they whispered among themselves, they were carrying huge bundles, which they set down at Mrs. Brewer's feet.

"Are you Mrs. Trask?" said the woman.

"No. I believe she's gone to the ship's hospital," said Mrs. Brewer. "Her daughter is ill."

The smiles disappeared.

"The page must have made a mistake," said one of the men.

The woman looked around anxiously. "We better get back to the ship's gangway. The boat is charging us by the minute."

She bent over to pick up her bundle, but Albert ran over and grabbed her arm. "Don't go. Mother will be here any minute. Oh—" He looked toward the door as Mother opened it for Uncle Clay, who was pushing Virginia in the wheelchair. "Here she is now."

As soon as the wheelchair stopped, Virginia jumped out. "What's the surprise, Bertie? Uncle Clay says you have a surprise for Mummy."

"It's his surprise too," said Albert.

"Albert thought of it," said Uncle Claybourne.

Virginia was impatient. "What is it?"

Sarah pushed Virginia aside. "I want to see too."

Nodding toward the bundles, Uncle Clay spoke to the merchants. "Are those—the tablecloths?"

"Tablecloths?" Mother repeated softly.

"Irish lace tablecloths," Albert said. "Just like the one you've always wanted."

The merchants were smiling again. One man was even rubbing his hands together. "Yes, missus," he said. "Finest lace there is."

"Sit down here, Kitty," Uncle Clay ordered. "You girls sit on the deck and stay out of the way."

The lady merchant had opened one of the bundles. "Yes, yes. Our lace is the best workmanship in Ireland. All handmade." She held one end of a cloth and a man took the other, stretching it out for several feet. "This one, for instance—"

"It's lovely, but—"

"Not what you're looking for, eh? Well, we have lots of them." The woman folded the first cloth and took out another.

Mother shook her head. Then suddenly—as one of

the men opened another bundle—her eyes brightened. "That one," she cried, pointing. "How big is that one?"

"Emm . . . that's a banquet, I think," said the man. He studied it. "Yes, three and a half meters."

The lady took the other side, and they held it to its full length. "It will seat twelve to fourteen," she said. "Beautiful pattern. See?" She handed the edge of it to Mother.

Mother rubbed her cheek gently with the lace. "Oh, it's just what I've always wanted. How much is it?"

Uncle Claybourne held his palms toward Mother's face. "It's a gift, Kitty. You don't ask the price of a gift."

But Albert was worried. He didn't know how much money Uncle Clay had from Grandmother or if his uncle would change his mind and expect Albert to work for him after all—maybe for even more than five years. He cleared his throat. "Yes, how much is it?"

"Just $325 in American money. Not much for lace this lovely."

"Three hundred and twenty-five dollars!" Emily exclaimed.

Mother pushed the tablecloth away. "That's too much. Show us something else."

It was Uncle Clay's turn to clear his throat. "You don't need to worry about money. I still have plenty left from Mama."

Mother's eyes widened. "But you said there wasn't enough for first-class tickets!"

Albert hurried to change the subject. "Is that the tablecloth you want, Mother?"

"Wel-l-l. It's very lovely."

"Good. I told Uncle Clay I was going to help pay for it. Because I'll be eating on it sometimes, of course."

"Then it's settled." Uncle Claybourne seemed eager to get back to his bridge game. While he pulled out his billfold and counted out the money for the two men, the lady merchant walked over to Mrs. Brewer.

"Maybe you'd like to see something?" she suggested.

Mrs. Brewer shook her head. "Oh, I don't think so. I couldn't afford it right now."

"We have smaller cloths. Less expensive patterns."

"No, no," said Mrs. Brewer. "Really."

With a shrug the lady closed up her bundle and headed to the door with the men.

Mother squeezed Albert's hand. "Oh, Bertie. How can I ever thank you!" She let go of his hand to brush the hair back on his forehead, and Albert could see her eyes misting. "Sometimes you remind me so much of your father, I almost feel he never left us." She turned away to pull a handkerchief from her purse.

Albert felt like shouting. He felt like lighting firecrackers. He felt like picking up Virginia and dancing her around the deck.

Now Uncle Clay started toward the door, but Mother called after him. "Thank you too, Clay."

"Don't thank me. It was Mama's money. And Albert's. And all Albert's idea. He was the one who knew the lace merchants were on board."

"He did not," Emily argued. "He didn't know anything until I told him."

Nine

Thursday, April 11, 1912.   1:25 P.M.

AWK! AWK! AWK!

"Look, Bertie!" Virginia tugged at the hem of his jacket and pointed out the window of C Deck Promenade. "It's like Piccadilly Circus. Except the pigeons are white."

Through the window Albert could see the hundreds of gulls as they flapped and pecked and scolded each other near the water below.

"They're not pigeons. They're gulls," Albert told his sister.

"What are they doing?"

"Fighting over my haddock almondine, I expect."

"Huh?" Ginny asked.

"The waste pipes of the ship are down there," Albert explained. "The cooks and dishwashers have probably scraped off the dishes from lunch, and the birds are fighting over all the luncheon food that I didn't get to eat."

"We got to eat our scones, though," Ginny said.

Albert made a face. *You* got to eat our scones, he thought.

All at once the ship's engines throbbed. The *Titanic* was ready to leave Queenstown and head to sea. Virginia grabbed Albert's arm to steady herself as the ship swung around in a huge quarter circle and skirted the Irish coast to the west.

AWK! AWK! A flurry of still-hungry gulls followed the ship, like kittens after their mother. Albert had never seen any birds like them.

"Do you want to play dolls with me?" said a small voice. Sarah, carrying a huge rag doll, was talking to Virginia.

"My doll's in our room," said Virginia. She crossed to the deck chair where Mother was sitting next to Mrs. Brewer. "Mummy, will you take me to get Elizabeth?"

"Don't you think you should lie down again?" Mother asked.

"No."

"Does your stomach still hurt?"

"No. I want to play. Let's go get my doll."

"All right. I want to take the tablecloth to the cabin anyway. Get in the wheelchair, and you can carry the tablecloth on your lap."

"No. The tablecloth has 'pendicitis. Put it in the wheelchair, and I'll push it."

"Oh, I don't think that's a good idea," Mother said. "The doctor doesn't want you to strain yourself. You climb in the chair and hold the tablecloth on your lap. There. Hold my satchel too."

The load looked awkward as Mother clumsily swung

the wheelchair around. Albert hurried after her. "I'll help you."

"I can manage. It's not far. We'll be right back."

Albert suddenly felt the urge to sketch. For the past twenty-four hours Virginia had upset the family so badly with her whining to stay in London and her imaginary ailments that he hadn't been able to explore the *Titanic* or sketch her or do any of the things he'd planned. But now his fingers itched to hold a pencil again. He wanted to set down all his impressions of this magnificent ship, beginning with her departure from Southampton yesterday. "Do you still have my sketch pad in your satchel?" he asked his mother.

She nodded and pulled his pad and pencils from her bag. Grinning with anticipation, Albert held the door for Mother to push the wheelchair through. But then, as she disappeared down the hallway, Albert's smile faded too.

Where could he go to sketch? He certainly couldn't do it here on C Deck Promenade—not with the entire Brewer family looking on. And there might be busybodies in the ship's library too. The only place where he'd be completely alone was in his own cabin, but he'd neglected to bring a key. Well, he'd just have to go back to the gentlemen's smoking room again and get a key from Uncle Clay.

He raced toward the stairs.

Thup, thup, thup. Someone was behind him. "Where are you going?" said a chirpy voice.

Oh, no, Albert thought. It was *her*. Miss Saints-and-Martyrs.

"Up," said Albert.

"I can see that. Up where?"

"Up by myself," he said pointedly.

"This is B Deck," she said when they'd climbed that far. "Is this where you're going?"

Actually, B Deck was exactly where he'd planned to go. But he couldn't give know-it-all Emily Brewer the satisfaction of being right again. "No." He kept climbing.

"A Deck?"

"No."

"You're not going to the boat deck, are you? It's too cold outside there."

"No one said you had to come with me."

"I don't have anyone else to talk to."

"You could read yourself a wonderful story about Saint Sebastian. Or recite some exciting poem in Latin."

"You don't mean that. You don't have to pretend with me, Albert Trask."

"Pretend what?"

"That you're rude and hateful. I know you're not. I saw how you skipped luncheon to stay with Virginia and how you helped pay for your mother's tablecloth."

Well, bully for you, Nosy-Nelly! Albert wanted to say. But instead of talking, he decided to climb the stairs two at a time. Maybe Emily wouldn't be able to keep up with him. The rest of the way he forced himself to maintain the pace, hoping she didn't know how hard he was panting.

Oof! The cold air took his remaining breath away. Just opening the door to the boat deck was like ramming his face into a bank of snow. Albert wished he'd been able to go back to the cabin for his overcoat and muffler. His only protections against the temperature were his cap and the suit jacket to his houndstooth knickerbockers. He pulled up the collar on his jacket.

Gasping, Emily followed him onto the deck and put on the coat she had been carrying over her arm. She nodded self-righteously as she looked at his upturned collar. "See, I told you it's too cold here. You should have brought a coat. There aren't even any passengers here, just that sailor there mopping the deck."

Albert faced her angrily. "All right. You've proved it once and for all. You can recite Latin. You're the only person in second class who knew about the lace merchants. You're the ship's expert on cold weather. You know everything in the whole world, and I'm a total idiot. Now there's nothing more you ever need to prove to me. You can just close your mouth and stop talking to me for the rest of your life."

"But I like to talk to you."

"Well, I like silence." He wasn't really sure he meant that. One of the things he hadn't liked about London was the fact that he had no friends his own age to talk to. Emily was twelve, *almost* his own age. But even if her voice didn't sound like fingernails scraped against wire screens (which it did), even if she didn't pretend to know everything in the entire world (which she did), even if she weren't the most mouthy person he'd ever met (which she was), Albert had never been friends with a girl.

But Emily had lost her papa, and Albert had that much in common with her. He even felt sorry for her, in a way. He had to feel sorry for someone so lonely for her father that she'd spend her whole life reading the world's two most dopey books just because they'd belonged to him.

67

Still, Albert's tongue kept on lashing out at her. "And if you're planning to stay where I am, you better be silent."

"But—"

He tore off a page of his sketch pad and handed it to her with a pencil. "I came up here to draw this ship, and that's what I'm going to do. So as long as you're not going to talk, you might as well draw something too."

He walked away from her, but she followed.

"I don't have anything to lean my paper against," she complained. "*You* have cardboard on your sketch pad."

"Sit on the deck and put your paper against it."

"It's too cold to sit on the deck."

"Then go to your cabin!"

Emily plunked herself down and sat cross-legged on the deck, her paper flat on the wooden flooring in front of her. "What shall I draw?"

"How should I know!"

AWK! AWK! AWK! Most of the gulls had fallen back, and a few others were still below, following the liner's waste pipes. But five or six now sailed overhead. Albert marveled at the grace with which they soared, hardly moving their wings up or down to maintain flight.

He pointed toward them. "You can draw those seagulls. Or Saint Sebastian full of arrows. Just keep your blooming mouth shut."

She did shut it, frowning, but Albert still heard noises. Laughter. He strained to listen. Sounds of merriment were coming from somewhere. He walked to the railing and looked down. Far astern, on the poop deck below, the third-class passengers were having a jolly time yelling and chasing each other. Then someone struck up an accordion, and several of the passengers began dancing an Irish jig.

Albert envied the fun they were having. He wished his family were traveling in third class. For a brief moment he was tempted to invite Emily over to show her that some people didn't think it was too cold on the open deck. But he quickly thought better of that. It would make him look weak—a sissy—to start a conversation with her now.

She'd already ruined his plan to sketch his impressions of the ship's departure yesterday. After all, he couldn't sketch anything strictly from memory with someone as obnoxious as Emily Brewer sitting practically next to him.

Then what *could* he draw?

Ah! One of the davits, a set of those intricate ropes and pulleys used to raise and lower the lifeboats to the ocean below. He was sure Emily would be impressed. She could never draw anything that technical.

He blew on his cupped hands to warm them and began working eagerly.

Ten

Emily walked over and stood beside Albert. "Well, I'm finished. Do you want to see my picture?" Whether he did or not, she thrust it under his nose.

It was a drawing of him, his cap on his head, his jacket collar upturned. He was holding his art tablet and looking up, as if to study something a distance away that he was sketching.

Albert noted the sense of movement she'd captured, the accuracy of the human form, and he resented her skill. The people he tried to draw always ended up stiff-looking and lifeless, like wooden puppets—or cadavers with rigor mortis. He wished his mother would take him seriously when he told her he wanted to take art lessons. "But you're going to be a lawyer," she'd always say. "Your grandmother expects you to take over your grandfather's firm when Claybourne retires."

He knew he should say something complimentary about Emily's drawing, but he couldn't bring himself to do it. "What did you draw me for?" he asked, handing the picture back.

She shrugged. "I don't know." She inspected the sketch herself for a minute, then rolled it up and slipped it into a pocket of her coat.

Albert closed the cover to his sketch pad. "It's a good picture," he said at last, grudgingly.

"I want to see your picture," Emily said.

"No."

"Please. I showed you mine."

Albert hesitated, then sighed and opened the cover, flipping through the pages to find the right one.

"Oh, not so fast. I want to see them all." She snatched the sketch pad and studied the pictures, pausing over each one. "Mmm—very nice," she'd say, or "not bad." When she'd gone through the notebook twice, she closed it and looked up at him. "Machines and buildings. Buildings and machines. Don't you like people?"

He seized the tablet from her. "Of course."

"You never draw them."

He'd thrown all of those drawings away. Trust Emily to notice. Darn her, he thought.

"I want to be an architect," he snapped. Not a lie. Not really. Grandmother Trask might be willing to pay for an art education if she thought he had some practical end in mind.

"Michelangelo and Leonardo were both architects," Emily pointed out, as if it were her duty to instruct him about things he'd known almost before she was born. "But they drew people too. Even sculpted them."

"So?"

"Adam, David, Moses, Virgin Mary—" Emily rattled on. Didn't she ever give things a rest?

"—Mona Lisa—" she continued.

He had to say something that would shut her up. "I guess I didn't meet anyone in London as interesting as the lady in the 'Mona Lisa' painting. Virginia and I spent all our time with a shriveled-up old tutor who looked as if she drank vinegar every afternoon at four o'clock instead of tea."

Emily giggled. "Oh, Albert, you're so funny!"

Funny? He liked being called funny.

"She sounds *very* interesting! A wonderful subject!" Emily squealed. "You should have drawn her!"

"She would have turned my paper red."

Emily seemed puzzled for a moment. "Oh, you mean her acid. Her pH." She burst into giggles again.

Albert couldn't help smiling too. He enjoyed telling jokes to someone who appreciated them.

He studied her pink cupid's-bow mouth, her petal-soft eyes, the trace of freckles on her nose. Right then—if he could draw people—he wouldn't have minded drawing Emily Brewer's face.

Looking up at him more seriously, Emily grasped his wrist. "Haven't you ever wanted to draw anyone?"

"No!" He pulled his arm free.

She stepped back, biting her lip. Awkwardness filled the silence that followed.

"I—I'm sorry," she said at last. "I didn't mean to criticize what you draw. You'll be a wonderful architect."

He cleared his throat. "My grandmother wants me to be a lawyer."

"Oh, I hope you won't give up drawing, though. You're a good artist."

With his free hand, he brushed at a crumb of something on his knickers. "Thank you. So are you."

"I especially like the sketch you did today, of the pulleys."

"Davits," Albert corrected.

"Davits? Is that what you call them?"

Albert nodded, pleased to change the subject. Pleased to talk about something he knew and Emily didn't. "Yes. They swing the lifeboats out from the ship's deck and then lower them into the water."

He balanced his pencil upright on an extended forefinger, then flipped it into the air and caught it on the same finger. It was a trick he'd mastered to amuse Virginia, and now he wondered if Emily were impressed too. She watched him without saying anything, so he slipped the pencil into the pocket of his knickers.

Emily looked over the railing. "I'll bet it's scary being lowered to the water in one of those boats."

"Yes," Albert agreed. "The *Titanic* is equal to eleven stories. That's a long way."

"Eleven stories!" Emily exclaimed. "I've never been in a building that tall, have you?"

Again he was pleased to show off his knowledge. "I've climbed to the top of the Washington Monument. That's equal to fifty stories."

"Fifty! Oh, my! What was it like up there?"

"You could see for miles. Maryland in one direction. Virginia in the other. But not as far as we can see here looking out over the water."

Silently the waves rocked them until Albert asked a

question that had been troubling him. "How many people do you think those lifeboats hold?"

"I don't know."

He nodded in the direction of the seaman on the deck. "Sometime when no one's around, I'd like to climb up on one of those boats and take the cover off and study it."

"How come?"

"Well—I overheard some women talking yesterday. One of them didn't think the ship has enough lifeboats to handle all the crew and passengers in case of an accident. I know the *Titanic* is unsinkable, and we won't have an accident—but I sort of thought it might be interesting to find out."

"Well, it certainly *would* be interesting to find out!" Emily charged off toward the seaman, who had finished his mopping and was now polishing the metal rail. Albert followed at her heels.

"How many people do those lifeboats hold?" she asked the crewman.

"Can't say as I know that, miss."

"Well, how many would you guess?" she persisted.

"Fifty, maybe, give or take a dozen. All the boats isn't exactly the same size."

"How many boats are there?" Albert asked.

"Sixteen regular ones. Eight in second class here. Eight more in first class." He pointed toward the bow of the ship. "They's some collapsible boats up that way too. Four of them."

"What about the third-class poop deck? Aren't there any lifeboats there?"

The seaman pulled off his hat to scratch his head with two grimy fingers. His nails, dirty as they were, had been chewed almost to the quick. "Never thought about that. Guess not." He grinned. "Lucky for those chaps this ship can't sink, I'd say."

"But if she did—the people in steerage—what would happen to them?" Emily demanded.

"Well, miss, I'm sure the officers would take care of things somehow. They'd unlock the barriers so third-class chaps could come here. Most likely."

Albert closed his eyes to multiply. "If there are twenty boats carrying an average of fifty people each, that's one thousand. The *Titanic* has a capacity for thirty-five hundred passengers and crew. Less than one-third of the people aboard could be saved in case of an accident."

"Ooh!" cried Emily. "That's disgraceful!"

"Hold up there. You young folks is going too fast. All ships on the White Star Line carry more lifeboats than the law requires."

Emily's voice was shrill. "More lifeboats than the law requires, but not enough to hold everyone aboard! Who makes those terrible laws, anyway?"

"Steady there, miss! What you don't understand is the purpose of lifeboats. They's just meant to ferry passengers to the rescue ships. Rescue ships come right fast now. It's not like in the old days before Mr. Marconi invented his wireless. Nowadays nearly every ship has a wireless operator on duty most of the time. Ten—twelve hours a day. Some ships, like this one we're on, has two messengers so they can work twenty-four hours. With a wireless they can send messages some two hundred miles. And there's bound to be a ship within that distance to come rescue folks before a liner sinks all the way down to Davy Jones's locker."

"I still think the law should be changed," Emily said. "There should be enough lifeboats to rescue everyone on a ship. Anything less is sinful."

"Well, if you're talking about the *Titanic*, you're forgetting two things, miss. First off, the ship is only two-thirds full. Assistant purser told me an hour ago they's some twenty-two hundred people aboard—passengers and crew. Second thing, everybody knows the *Titanic* is built so she can't sink. That's why me wife begged me to sign on. Said she'd feel better home alone with the little ones knowing I was on a ship that can't sink."

"But what if it does?" Emily persisted. "What if something unexpected happens? There aren't even half enough boats for twenty-two hundred people."

The crewman pulled off his hat, wiped his forehead with the inside of a bent elbow, and leaned toward her. "I'll tell you something if you promise not to whisper it about. I've been kind of wondering about that meself. Usually on most ships I sign up on, the captains hold drills right away so's the chaps on board will know exactly what to do in case of trouble. But Captain Smith—he's a good man, and I'm not saying anything against him, mind you—hasn't posted no notice yet about a drill."

"You mean—" Emily began.

"Uh-oh," the seaman interrupted. "Here comes Fifth Officer Lowe, and me work's not done."

The approaching officer was young—late twenties, Albert would guess—but he had a fierce look.

"Lowe's a tough one, he is," whispered the crewman. "I can't talk to you young folks no more."

Eleven

"If we ever take another ocean trip, can't we please go third class?" Albert asked.

Mother wiped her mouth daintily with a linen napkin and set it beside her plate. "Third class? Oh, Bertie. Don't be ridiculous." She put both hands on the table as if to push her chair back.

"I mean it, Mother. Please."

"Do you have any idea what things are like in steerage? Ladies' and gentlemen's rooms too far away to reach if you're having an emergency at night. Not enough showers. People stacked in sleeping quarters like logs on their way to a sawmill. I can just imagine what it smells like down there."

"I'm sure third class is nice on the *Titanic*, Mother. The people dance and sing. They're having fun."

"Really? Well, I'll just have to write to Anna Skaggs and ask her how much fun she had."

"Who's Anna Skaggs?" Albert asked.

"A suffragette I met at Zora's. She's below on the *Titanic* right this minute. Bought a third-class ticket as a matter of principle, she said. Even Zora thought she was crazy."

Dishes clattered as the dining saloon stewards cleared off the breakfast tables. Mother started to rise.

"Sit down please, Katherine," said Uncle Clay. "I need to talk to you."

"Can't it wait? I promised to join Mrs. Brewer on the C Deck Promenade. We were in the middle of a discussion."

Albert could see the backs of the Brewer family as they headed toward the door. They had just left the table, and Virginia was trotting to keep up with Sarah. Weird as the Brewer family was, Ginny's new friend had brought a wonderful change in his sister. She'd stopped whining for Miss Harcher or inventing stomach pains to get her own way, and the wheelchair had been returned to the ship's hospital.

"It's important, Katherine," Uncle Clay said.

So was my conversation, Albert thought, and I was talking to Mother first. "You'd be surprised about third class, Mother," he continued. "The families—"

"Albert!" said Uncle Claybourne. "You are interrupting!"

Why did adults always think that young people were the only ones who interrupted?

"Something Mama wants me to settle with you, Kitty."

78

Uncle Clay combed his mustache with two fingers, as he always seemed to do when he was troubled about something. "We need to talk about it before we get home."

Mother grinned. "Oh, dear. Sounds ominous."

Uncle Claybourne sat in the chair Mrs. Brewer had vacated next to Mother and brushed at some crumbs resting on the table. "I hope you won't think so when you hear what it is."

"Well, tell me quickly then. I don't want to be rude and break my promise."

"This isn't something we can discuss quickly, Kitty. Albert, run ahead and tell Mrs. Brewer that your mother has been detained."

"Uh—yessir," Albert said, but he made no effort to stand up. If Grandmother's business was as important as Uncle Clay said, Albert wanted to hear it too.

"All right, Clay. What is it?" Mother asked.

He picked up a crumb and studied it. "How would you like a new house?"

"A new house?" she said. "But I like the one I have. And it's so near to the shops at Dupont Circle. It's even within walking distance of the bigger stores on F Street."

"Yes," said Uncle Clay, leaning forward. Albert could imagine him interrogating a witness on the stand. "But wouldn't you like a new house? A bigger one? Mama's offering to build you a bigger one. And provide servants to take care of it."

Mother backed away from his face, which he'd pushed almost next to hers. "Somehow I suspect there's a condition attached to this."

"There's no condition . . . exactly."

79

"All right. What is it?"

"She just wants to build it in McLean. On her property. She has fourteen acres, you know. Lots of room."

"I suspected as much."

"Well, she's getting old, Kitty. With Mason gone now, she wants to spend her last few years near her grandchildren. Albert and Virginia love it out there in the country."

Albert felt the need to clarify his position. "We love it to visit. On the weekends and in the summer. Not to live there. Where would I go to school? I don't want to be tutored again."

Uncle Claybourne crushed the crumb he was holding, and tiny particles fell slowly to the table like specks of dust. "I thought you were taking a message to Mrs. Brewer, Albert."

Mother moistened her lips with her tongue and nodded toward the door. "Yes, Bertie. Run along."

"Yes, ma'am." Reluctantly he rose and started toward the door, sucking the insides of his cheeks and clenching his hands inside the pockets of his knickers until his fingernails carved into his flesh. He was the man of the family now. He should be included in important decisions like this one.

On the C Deck Promenade he saw Virginia playing paper dolls on the floor with Sarah and Emily. Albert kicked his toe against the deck, realizing what it was that he had hated most about England. It wasn't the biting cold or the gray skies or even the coal smoke in the air that made his chest hurt when he tried to run. It was being tutored. It was never going to places where he could make friends, never playing games with other boys.

Mrs. Brewer looked up. "Where's your mother?"

"She asked to be excused for a while. She had some business to discuss with Uncle Claybourne."

"Oh. Well . . ." said Mrs. Brewer. "I've been trying to remember the name of the gentleman in Baltimore she asked me about."

Mother and Mrs. Brewer had begun a lively conversation at breakfast. Over spicy sausages and eggs Benedict with ham and stewed tomatoes sprinkled with sugar and paprika, they had discovered that the Brewers were returning to Baltimore, where Mother was born, and they spent the meal trying to identify any mutual friends.

"You don't remember who it was, do you?" Mrs. Brewer asked Albert.

"I'm afraid not, ma'am."

"Then I'll just have to wait until she gets here." She turned to her daughters and Virginia. "Aren't you girls cold sitting on the deck?"

"No, ma'am," said Emily.

"Well, if you get cold, come sit on the chairs."

"Yes, ma'am."

Albert walked over to the side of the ship and looked out the window. The sky was cloudless. Bright sunlight danced on the water like flickers of candlelight on crystal. He watched the swells of ocean, rolling and rolling, until the motion made him dizzy. He didn't even realize Mother and Uncle Claybourne had rejoined the group until he heard Mother's voice behind him.

"It was Clifton Weaver," Mother was saying to Mrs. Brewer. "Did you ever meet a Dr. Clifton Weaver?"

Albert spun around, examining Mother's face for a clue about how her discussion with Uncle Claybourne had ended, but he could read nothing.

"Is he a clergyman? As missionaries we've met most of the clergy in Baltimore," said Mrs. Brewer.

Uncle Claybourne paced for a minute and then took the chair next to Mother's. He seemed tense. Was the argument over? Had Mother won?

"No, a medical doctor," said Mother. "He took his training in Washington, and my husband did some legal work for him there. I understand he has a fine practice in Baltimore now and teaches part-time at the new medical school, Johns Hopkins. He might be someone you'd want to consult about Robert."

At the mention of his name, little Robert stirred on his mother's lap. His papery skin seemed unusually sallow this morning, almost green, and there were dark circles under both eyes. It was odd the way he never cried or murmured, just languished on his mother's lap like seaweed growing listlessly in her arms.

Footsteps tapped along the deck, and Albert looked up to see Colonel Heath, a gentleman who had been very attentive to Mother at dinner last night, walking toward them. Even at this hour of the morning he looked every inch the proper gentleman, from the ascot tie around his neck to the gray spats protecting his shoes.

Uncle Clay leaned forward in his deck chair, eyeing the colonel suspiciously, like one of the guards of the crown jewels in the Tower of London. There was a V-shaped furrow in Uncle Clay's forehead, which made him look older. And his mouth, which showed splendid teeth like Father's on those rare occasions when he smiled, was drawn into a tight, ugly line.

Maybe he was angry because his conversation with Mother about moving to Virginia hadn't gone the way he'd hoped. But maybe—probably, Albert suspected—he was still angry about last night. In her low-cut satin gown and feather boa Mother had looked particularly lovely at dinner, and several gentlemen had come to the Trasks' table and introduced themselves. One of them was Colonel Heath from California, who asked Mother if she and her family wouldn't like to see his stereopticon slides of his trip up the Nile River to the pyramids at Giza. But as soon as the family went to the second-class library and Colonel Heath opened his projector case, Uncle Claybourne started drumming his blunt-edged fingers on the arms of his chair as if it were already time to call the evening to a halt.

Now the colonel bowed low, took Mother's hand, and kissed it. Turning to Uncle Clay, he said, "Ah, Mr. Trask. Would you mind if I took your lovely sister-in-law for a stroll?"

Albert's uncle tipped his head stiffly to one side. "As a matter of fact I was just about to take her on a stroll myself. We have some family business we need to settle."

The colonel kissed Mother's hand again. "Well then— another time." He turned and left.

At that Uncle Claybourne rose. "Come, please, Kitty. Albert, we may be a while. Perhaps you should take Virginia to her cabin."

Ginny's huge hair ribbon bobbed in protest. "I want to stay with Sarah. Emily's showing us how to make paper dolls. Mayn't I stay, Mum? Please?"

"All right. If Mrs. Brewer doesn't mind."

"Of course not," said Mrs. Brewer. "Emily will keep an eye on the girls."

Mother held herself proudly as she walked to the door

beside Uncle Clay, but the slender figure in the hobble skirt was so much smaller that Albert wondered how she could protect herself. Uncle Clay wasn't going to give up. From now on he and Grandmother Trask would try to make all the decisions that Mother should be making— all the decisions that Mother and *Albert* should be making.

No wonder Mother hadn't wanted to go home.

Twelve

What could be taking Mother and Uncle Claybourne so long?

Virginia and Sarah had long ago put away their paper dolls and were sitting beside Emily in a deck chair as she read aloud:

The wicked stepmother could see that her husband cared about no one so much as his children. She became so angry that she packed up all her belongings in a large red handkerchief. Then she ran away and never came back, and Hansel and Gretel and their good father lived happily ever after.

"Read us another one," said Sarah.

"Yes, please, Emily," said Virginia. "Read us another one from that book, not the book about martyrs. I like stories where the people live happily ever after."

"My throat's dry," said Emily. "I can't read anymore right now. Shall we trade, Mama? I can take Robert for a while."

"Shh. He's asleep," said Mrs. Brewer. She stood and laid the boy gently in her deck chair, covering him with the blanket she'd brought from her cabin. Albert watched the two of them leaning over the frail boy, Emily a youthful version of her sad-eyed mother. He liked the way Emily's freckles spilled from her nose onto her cheeks, like sprinkles of red pepper.

Albert cleared his throat. "Would you like to go up to the boat deck with me and—look around?"

"I don't have time to play," Emily said. "Can't you see I'm helping my mother?"

Albert suddenly felt hollow. He had thought Emily liked him, that she had enjoyed being with him yesterday. But now she was treating him the way she had done at first, as if he were stupid. He wished he had taken Virginia to her cabin long ago, as Uncle Claybourne had suggested.

"Oh, run along and enjoy yourself for a minute," said Mrs. Brewer. "I'll watch the girls while Robert's asleep. But don't stay long. He'll wake up soon."

"You're sure it's all right if I go?"

"Yes. But not too long."

Emily smiled and headed toward Albert. He wanted to tell her not to bother, that he could go to the boat deck perfectly well alone. But the truth was that he was eager for any company, even hers. And he was flattered by Emily's smile, even if he would have torn up his art book and sworn never to sketch another picture again in his whole life before he'd admit it out loud.

They started up the red-carpeted stairs. Finally he turned and spoke, partly to vent his anger, partly because he was curious. "Don't you ever get tired of being helpful? Don't you ever think it might be nice to have fun for a change? To do what you want to do?"

"Sometimes, I guess. But I read a lot while I'm tending Sarah and Robert. And I think it's fun to help people."

They climbed the rest of the way to the boat deck and went through the door. "Now *that's* fun," Albert said, pointing.

"What?"

"Listen," said Albert.

"What?"

"Can't you hear those people down there?" He led her to the railing at the stern and pointed to the third-class passengers who were singing and dancing on the poop deck aft. "They don't even care that it's cold because they're having so much fun."

"Well, I'm having fun too," said Emily. "I like talking to you."

He looked into her eyes. Soft. Brown. Flecked with green. Then he felt embarrassed and turned away. "Baltimore isn't very far from Washington," he said. "Less than two hours on the train. Uncle Claybourne sometimes goes there to court. Maybe we'll see each other when we get back to America."

"Maybe. If the doctors can help Robert." For a minute she studied the toe of a high-buttoned brown shoe as she twisted its sole against the wooden deck. "Well, what did we come to the boat deck for? To look inside the life-boats? We can't look inside the covers now, with all those people around."

There were eight or ten other second-class passengers on the deck, most of them walking briskly to keep warm.

"I guess not," Albert said.

"What shall we do then?"

Watching the third-class passengers no longer interested him. "Nothing, I guess."

"Well, I'd better go back and help Mama with Sarah and Robert."

"All right."

Silently they walked side by side down the stairs, but when they got to C Deck, Albert turned toward the door to the second-class library. "Tell Virginia I'll be there in a minute. I'm going to see if I can find a book to read."

"Don't hurry. I'll watch her."

Albert pushed open the door to the library. This was where his family had come last night to see Colonel Heath's stereopticon slides, but the room looked different in daylight. On one of the sycamore-paneled walls was a huge open fireplace. Above it hung an oil painting of sailing ships at sea. A clock rested on the mantel.

Walking into the room, Albert was surprised to see Mother writing in her journal at one of the Duncan Phyfe tables. Good. Uncle Claybourne was no longer with her. Albert could talk to her alone.

"Mother—" he began.

She looked up, startled, then quickly closed the cover so he couldn't see the writing. Her cheeks looked red. Had she been crying?

"Are you all right?" he asked.

"Of course."

"Did you—uh—get the problem settled?"

"What problem?"

"With Uncle Clay. About moving to McLean." He rubbed his sweaty hands against the sides of his knickers. "I'd—I'd prefer to stay in Washington, ma'am."

"Yes-s-s. And I'd prefer to stay in London." Mother looked down, screwing the lid onto her fountain pen and setting the pen on the table. "But it will be nice for Virginia, at least, in McLean."

Albert's words came out in a rush. "No, Mother, no. Virginia would be better off in Washington too. She needs friends her own age to play with. Haven't you noticed how much happier she's been since she met Sarah? And I need the chance to study art and play sports in school. We both need a real school."

Mother's eyes glistened in the light. She *had* been crying. "Well then, maybe you'll be happy to know that your grandmother is prepared to take care of part of your problem too. Your uncle has persuaded her to send you to a boarding school in Virginia during the week. A military boarding school."

Military boarding school? Albert felt dizzy. Once he had overheard Uncle Claybourne talking to Father. "That son of yours is soft, Mason. Katherine treats him like a girl. Taking him to the theater. Allowing him to draw all the time. You've got to toughen him up before we let him into this law firm. Military school is what he needs. A good dose of discipline."

Albert sank to a chair. "Oh, Mother, please don't let them do that to me. Please."

"I wish I could help you, Bertie, but you at least have a choice. Tutor or military school. That's more than they offered me."

He leaned forward. "What do you mean?"

"We either move to McLean or Mother Trask cuts off the annuity." Her voice broke, and she reached for the lace handkerchief on the table, a new one Albert had given her for her birthday, which already looked wrinkled and damp.

"Who cares?" The table shook as Albert slammed his hand on it. "We don't need her old annuity! You can get a job. Lots of women have jobs."

"Doing what? Selling ribbons at Woolworth's? I wouldn't make enough to feed myself, let alone you and Ginny."

"How about working as a nurse in a hospital? Or teaching? I know they don't let married ladies teach school, but widows can do it."

"You need special training to do those things. My schooling at the Maryland Institute didn't prepare me to work. I'd have to go back to a university. At least two years. How would we live while I'm doing that?"

"I'd help out. I'd get a job. While you're learning."

For an answer, she just shook her head and blew her nose on the soiled handkerchief.

"How about sewing for people? You made that wonderful costume for Miss LaRue. Designed it yourself. You could be a seamstress."

"I might enjoy that for a few months, but I couldn't do it for the rest of my life. Sewing makes me nervous after a while."

A new idea occurred to him. Why hadn't he thought of it before? "An actress! You've always wanted to be one. Miss LaRue arranged that tryout for you with the director she knew in London. You could be an actress in Washington."

"You need connections to get acting jobs these days, Bertie."

"Grandmother has lots of connections."

Mother snorted. "Do you really think she'd use them to help me become an actress? She sent for us to come home from London because she didn't want me even spending time with one. Because she wanted to keep her eye on me." She stood up. "I'm sorry, Bertie. I'm afraid we have to move to McLean. But at least you have the opportunity to choose between military school and a tutor."

Albert rose to his feet and caught her arm. "No, Mother! Don't give up! Please!"

She put her hand over his and squeezed it. "I'm afraid it's hopeless."

"No, it isn't! I'll think of something."

She shook her head again. Then, with a sigh, she stuffed her personal belongings and writing equipment from the table into her satchel and started to the door, looking almost as crumpled as her lace handkerchief.

Albert reached into his pocket and rubbed the dented cover of Father's watch. He knew he could think of something if he tried hard enough. He had to!

Thirteen

Sunday, April 14, 1912.   10:05 A.M.

After his talk with Mother on Friday Albert had figured out the answer to their problems. There was to be a Sunday worship service this morning in the first-class section of the ship that anyone could attend, and Albert had lain awake for two nights, planning how he'd meet Mr. Harry Gordon, the theatrical producer, to tell him about Mother. If Mr. Gordon would use his connections to help her find a job in Washington designing and sewing costumes until she knew how to be an actress, Mother could support the family at a job she wanted to do. And Albert could go on living and attending school in Washington with his old friends.

Mr. Gordon would surely help Mother find a job, wouldn't he? And Grandmother Trask couldn't stop them from living in Washington then, could she?

Now in the light of day, when it was almost time for

the service, Albert's stomach jumped like a grasshopper as he worried about how he'd find Mr. Gordon in the crowd and what he'd say to him first.

He was also worried about what kind of impression he'd make on a famous theatrical producer if he couldn't get his stupid necktie to hang right. Today, because it was Sunday, he was wearing long trousers in the daytime for the first time in his life. He wanted to look good. He yanked his knot undone, grateful that the Brewers were late in coming to pick him up.

The Brewers hadn't come to breakfast. According to Georgie, who was the cabin steward for both families, little Robert hadn't slept well the previous night so Mrs. Brewer wanted him to stay in bed this morning and rest up for the church service. It was to be at 10:30 in the first-class dining saloon on D Deck. Other services were being held in second- and third-class sections of the ship this morning, but without telling anyone that he was planning to meet Mr. Gordon, Albert had persuaded his family and the Brewers to attend the one in first class and had arranged with Georgie to lead them there.

Albert finished retying his necktie. Mmm. A little better this time. In his new outfit he actually looked pretty good—except for a danged pimple that was forming on the side of his nose. He wished there were no such thing as pimples. He wished his nose weren't so big. He wished he looked more like Father. Or Mother, for that matter. He hadn't inherited the coloring of either of his parents— Mother's dark hair and fair skin or Father's reddish-blond hair and tanned complexion. Albert's coloring was drab. Nothing anyone would notice. But his hair was thick and wavy. Mother once told him that girls were attracted to boys with wavy hair. He wondered if Emily Brewer was.

Just for the heck of it, he opened Uncle Claybourne's bottle of sweet-smelling tonic and combed his hair with it. He practiced holding his head different ways to see which view looked best. He practiced smiling, showing off his good teeth.

From his vest pocket he pulled out Father's watch and read the time: 10:10. Absentmindedly he tried to snap the cover shut, forgetting for an instant that his bratty sister had ruined the most valuable thing he'd ever owned.

A knock sounded at the door. Albert took a deep breath and opened it.

"Well, ye're ready for service, are ye?" said Georgie.

Behind the cabin steward stood the Brewer family, who had come with him. They were all dressed in white, like a family of angels.

"Yes, I'm ready," Albert said out loud. At least he hoped he was.

"Well, I'm to take you and the Brewers to meet your mum and them. They's waiting outside the reception room to the dining saloon, by the first-class lifts."

Albert nodded and shut the door behind him, falling into step beside Emily, who was holding Sarah's hand. Emily had a pale pink ribbon in her hair and a tiny gold locket around her neck. She smelled nice.

Just ahead, Mrs. Brewer was panting as she walked beside Georgie. "How far is it?"

"Right here on D Deck, it is. Not far if we could go direct. But we has to go 'round and about these little corridors to get to the gate. A steward's on duty this morning to open it and let folks through for the service. Here, let me carry your boy for you," Georgie offered.

"Oh, thank you," said Mrs. Brewer, handing Robert over. "He does get heavy sometimes."

Georgie turned his head a bit to include Albert and the girls in his monologue. "Lots of stewards still don't know their ways about this ship. But me, I learned first thing with me papa's help. It's hard to find your way about unless there's someone to show you, especially when the gates is locked between the classes. The stewards to unlock them will only be on duty for a few minutes after the service, so you best prance right along afterward and hurry back to second class. Wouldn't want to get stuck there with them fancy millionaires, I expect." Georgie laughed loudly, as if he'd told a wonderful joke.

"Hmmph," said Emily.

They threaded their way through the corridors until Georgie pointed with his forehead. "There the gate is now."

"Why do rich people lock us out?" asked Sarah.

"Because they don't know what it says in the Bible about rich men getting into heaven," said Emily.

Smiling, the first-class steward held the door open, and Georgie led the way again through more corridors until they reached the most beautiful foyer Albert had ever seen. Staircases of polished oak swept gracefully in two directions. Crystal chandeliers sparkled from above.

"Well, there's Mrs. Trask with Miss Virginia. And Mr. Trask too." Georgie set little Robert on the floor. "So, lad, can ye stand up for a bit?"

"I seepy," said Robert.

He started to lie down on the marble floor, but Mrs. Brewer scooped him up in her arms. "Thank you, Georgie."

"Yes, thank you for bringing us," Albert called over his shoulder as he walked toward Mother.

Mother's nod included all of them before she spoke to Mrs. Brewer. "How lovely your family looks. That's a beautiful brooch. Is it an heirloom?"

"Yes. Thank you. My grandmother's."

"It's exquisite."

Mother was wearing the purple suit and plumed hat she'd worn when they left London, but now she had on a new shirtwaist trimmed with lace. Her raven hair puffed becomingly around her face.

"Oh, dear," she said, turning to Albert. "Your necktie is crooked. Here, let me retie it for you."

Not here, Albert thought. Not in front of the Brewers, and those fancy-looking people over there. One of them might even be Mr. Harry Gordon. But he was afraid he'd create an ever bigger scene if he protested, so he stood still, letting Mother treat him like a child.

Trying to keep his back toward Emily, he studied the magnificent wall carvings, the gilded balustrades. Once, when Father was entertaining a wealthy out-of-town client, the adults had taken Albert and the man's son to lunch at the Willard Hotel in Washington. At the time Albert had thought it must be the most splendid place in the entire world, but nothing about it could compare to the elegance of this first-class foyer on the *Titanic*.

Mother stood back and looked at his necktie. "There," she said. "That's better."

Albert's palms felt wet. But maybe too many people hadn't noticed his mother fussing over him. The first-class passengers seemed to be paying attention only to their friends. And Emily had taken Sarah and Virginia a few feet away to look at a wooden cupid, as tall as Robert.

"Come back, Emily. Stay with us," Mrs. Brewer called, and Emily brought her sister and Virginia back to huddle with the other Brewers and Trasks near the first-class elevators.

The door to one of the lifts opened, and Albert almost gasped out loud as he saw the couple inside. Helping his wife off the elevator was Colonel John Jacob Astor, whose picture Albert had seen scores of times in newspapers and magazines. Albert would have known that oval face anywhere—the drooping mustache, the cleft chin, the heavy brows. His new bride looked even younger in person than she did in the newspapers. Hardly older than Emily.

One hand holding her husband's arm, her chin held high in the air, Mrs. Astor walked straight toward the Trasks and Brewers as if she planned to speak to them, which of course she didn't. Instead, she just kept walking, like Moses parting the waters of the Red Sea.

The adults realized at once what was expected. Mother seized Albert and Virginia with either hand and stepped to one side with Uncle Claybourne. Mrs. Brewer stepped to the other side with her family, making a pathway for America's regal couple.

As the Astors strutted through the reception room toward the adjoining dining saloon, Albert watched in awe. He wished he dared catch up with them and speak to the colonel: "Do you know Mr. Harry Gordon? Would you introduce me to him?"

But Emily was not impressed. "Hmmph," she sneered. "Who does that lady think she is?"

"That's Mrs. John Jacob Astor, wife of the colonel," Albert explained. "He bought her the lace bed jacket in Queenstown."

"So?"

"Have you ever heard of the Waldorf-Astoria?"

"No."

"It's the fanciest hotel in New York. The colonel owns it. And lots of other famous buildings too. He's one of the richest men in the world."

"Well, he and his snooty wife don't own me," said Emily.

Uncle Claybourne brushed a bit of lint from his lapel. "I don't suppose anyone will ever own you, young lady. Including your husband—if you're ever able to catch one."

"Especially not my husband," said Emily. "And I'll catch one if I feel like it."

Mother's gaze was on the doorway through which the Astors had disappeared. She waved her hand toward it, giggling. "She's—she's *enceinte*!"

"That's nice," said Mrs. Brewer.

"*Nice* may not be exactly the right word," said Uncle Clay.

"What's *on sont*?" asked Virginia.

Mother made a face at her. "Ssh."

Albert pulled his sweaty hands from his pockets and tugged at his collar. Sarah and Virginia wouldn't understand this conversation, of course, but he did. He wished he could disappear through the fancy marble flooring and never be seen again.

"What's *on sont*?" Virginia repeated.

Mother put her hand on Ginny's shoulder. "Hush,

dear. Nothing you need to know about until you're older."

Albert sneaked a look at Emily to see if she were as uncomfortable as he was, but she seemed unperturbed.

"Why isn't it nice, Mr. Trask?" said Mrs. Brewer.

"I was referring to the scandal. Colonel Astor's disgraceful divorce was in all the newspapers a few years ago. I guess you were in Ceylon then. And two years later he turned around and married a woman younger than his son. Eighteen. She couldn't be more than nineteen now."

Sarah tugged at her sister's skirt. "What does *on sont* mean?"

"It's French for being with child, like Mary in the Bible," explained Emily. "It means a lady is going to have a baby."

"Oh, is that all. The ladies in Ceylon are always having babies," Sarah explained to Virginia. "Mama and Emily used to go help them get born." She took Ginny's hand. "Come on, let's skip."

Albert took out his handkerchief and pretended to blow his nose, too embarrassed to look at Emily again. Then he realized the others had left him behind, and he hurried to catch up.

Like the reception room next to it, the first-class dining saloon was paneled in white. Tables had been pushed aside to make room for two kinds of chairs, now serving as pews. Green upholstered armchairs were set up in front, and wicker chairs—possibly from the reception room—were arranged in back. Walking on the thick carpet was like walking on fur.

Many worshippers had already gathered in the huge room, separating themselves into three distinct groups.

Expensively clad men and women sat in the front, talking cheerfully to one another. Toward the back another group sat more quietly with hands folded in their laps. Against the wall—even though not all the wicker chairs were occupied—a third group of people stood crowded together. They seemed ill at ease, almost apologetic at being caught in this magnificent room with the richly carved alcoves and leaded windows. Members of the ship's orchestra sat facing the worshippers as they played a solemn hymn.

Uncle Clay spotted a cluster of empty seats about three rows from the back and motioned to the others to follow him.

"Save me a seat," Albert called with a wave. "I'll be right back."

Heading toward the front of the room, he took a deep breath as he looked among the people seated on the green chairs for a friendly face he might approach. Good, he thought. There, on the aisle, were two young men in their late teens or early twenties. He balled his fists in his pockets and walked toward them.

"Do you know Mr. Harry Gordon?" he asked the closer man.

"Doesn't everyone?"

Albert let that pass. "Would you point him out to me?"

"You mean now?"

"Yes, please."

"I haven't seen him this morning. I don't think he's here."

"Of course not," said the second man. "He wouldn't dare show his face among all these women from second and third class. He'd be mobbed to death by Irish parlor-maids looking for jobs as chorus girls."

Inside his pockets Albert tightened his fists. What right did this man have to say who should or shouldn't be an actress? "Are you sure he isn't here? Would you mind standing up and taking a better look?"

Albert smelled perfume. He turned to see Emily standing next to him.

"Your mother said for me to come get you," Emily chirped in her high voice. "She can't save your seat any longer."

"That's all right. I'll stand. Tell her I'll be there in a minute."

Someone grabbed his arm. An officer with slitty eyes. "Are you a first-class passenger?"

"N-n-no, sir."

"This part of the room is for first class only. You get back where you belong. The service is about to begin."

"Come on," Emily whispered.

"But—"

Just then a distinguished old gentleman with a gray beard stood up in front, ready to begin the service. From pictures he'd seen, Albert knew it was Captain Smith, looking as saintly as a white-suited Santa Claus in his snowy dress uniform.

Emily tugged at Albert's jacket. "Come on," she insisted.

Albert looked from Emily to Captain Smith, reluctant to go back to his seat but knowing he couldn't try to find Harry Gordon during the service. He shrugged and followed Emily to his wicker chair.

Before sitting, he picked up the prayer book resting there. Not the *Book of Common Prayer* Albert was familiar with, but the White Star Company's own prayer book. He liked the feel of it in his hands and the sound of Captain Smith's rich, confident voice as he read the service. He sang enthusiastically with the congregation and string orchestra.

After the service was over, Albert stood up to look for Mr. Gordon again. People seemed unwilling to leave, and most of them were talking at once. Ladies in silks and feathers. Men in woolens and gloves. As dining saloon stewards weaved around the passengers, trying to move the furniture back in place, Albert elbowed forward. Someone clamped him on the shoulder. One of the dining stewards.

"You're going the wrong way, lad. Out the door now, please. Me and the other stewards has got to get these tables back where they belong so we can serve luncheon."

"But—but I want to talk to someone. Someone in first class."

"Not in this room, lad. We's got to clear everyone out of here. Go to the reception room."

Other stewards had apparently spoken to the first- and third-class passengers because everyone was leaving now, heading in the same direction toward the reception room. Albert sighed with relief. Maybe he could talk to Harry Gordon there.

But in the reception area, the passengers were separating again into groups. One cabin steward was waving an umbrella in the air and telling the third-class passengers to follow him. Another cabin steward was waving a cane and shouting. "All second-class passengers follow me.

The barrier will be locked in five minutes. Second-class passengers follow me."

"Oh!" Mother said breathlessly. "I've got to get out of here. I'm getting crushed."

For once, little Robert started to cry.

"Hush, dear," said Mrs. Brewer.

"Maybe lunch is ready in our own dining saloon," said Emily.

"I'm hungry," said Sarah.

"Come on, Bertie," said Virginia. "Let's go to the deck and order tea and scones."

Albert looked toward the first-class passengers who seemed in no hurry to leave the reception area. He'd come this far, and he wasn't leaving, not before talking to Harry Gordon.

But Uncle Claybourne nudged him forward, speaking firmly. "Albert! It's time to go!"

Darn Uncle Clay! Albert thought angrily. Darn all the rules on this ship! How could he ever find a job for Mother, how could he keep his family together in Washington, if no one would even let him talk to Mr. Gordon?

Fourteen

The gate to the first-class area on D Deck was easy to find a second time. Albert looked over his shoulder to see if anyone was watching, then pulled the manicure kit from his pocket and unsnapped it.

He'd seen Mattie Lou's husband pick the lock on Grandmother's house once when Mattie Lou had accidentally shut the three of them outside, so he knew it could be done. Of course he didn't have the same kinds of picks Abraham had used. But he felt sure one of the pointy tools Uncle Claybourne used on his fingernails and cuticles should work. For starters he decided to try the one with the sharpest point. He removed it and put the kit back in his pocket.

"Hey there, young chap! Just what do ye think ye're doing?"

Looking up, Albert saw a cabin steward frowning at him. Older than Georgie. Broader shoulders.

Albert hid the tool behind his back. "Uh—" He'd rehearsed his alibi in his mind in case he got caught, but the words didn't come out as smoothly as he'd planned. He wasn't used to lying. "I—I'm lost. All these pathways. They look alike."

"So ye thought maybe ye'd take a shortcut through first class?"

Albert ignored the sarcasm. "Yessir."

"And just what would the cabin be that ye're looking for?"

"Uh—it's right on this deck, sir. D 68."

"Well, ye won't find D 68 by going through first class, ye won't. It's back behind. Come with me, and I'll walk ye there."

To make sure Albert stayed with him, the steward rested a firm hand on his shoulder, their footsteps *clip-clop*ping on the linoleum as they walked through the maze of narrow corridors.

"Right there, ye be." The steward nodded toward D 68.

"Yessir. Thank you, sir." Albert stuffed the tool from the manicure kit into one pocket and pulled out his cabin key from another.

Too stubborn to leave, the steward watched until Albert had unlocked the door.

Albert waved back through the doorway and called, "Thanks again."

"Um-hmm."

Albert closed the door. Hardly breathing, he rested his

ear against the wall until the *clip-clop* of retreating foot-steps faded and died. Then he cautiously opened the door again and looked both ways. Good. No one was in sight.

He locked the door behind him, jogged to the lift, and pushed the button. There were still five decks on this ship with who knew how many gates separating the first- and second-class areas. One of them was sure to have a lock that he could pick, and he'd try them all if he had to. But now it was getting late, and Mother would soon start worrying about him. The only barrier he'd have time to try tonight was the other one he'd already seen and could find quickly—the one on the boat deck.

Actually, he'd have to go through two barriers on the boat deck because the officers' section in the middle of the deck separated the first-class bow and the second-class stern areas. But he wouldn't even need to pick the locks on the gates because he knew the boat deck barriers would be easy for him to crawl through—if no one was about. He was pretty sure there wouldn't be any passengers on the boat deck right then because the day had been so cold. Of course some officers might be working in their own area, but he'd just have to sneak past them.

He got off the lift and opened the door to the deck. "Ooh!" he mumbled to himself. He'd sure been right about the temperature up here. But he'd been wrong to think he might have the second-class passenger area to himself. A couple with a young child was going for a stroll, and two officers were talking together near one of the lifeboats. Why didn't they all go inside where it was warm, for heck's sake?

Albert wandered over to the railing, pretending to be interested in the ocean below. Shivering, he turned up the collar on his jacket and then rammed his hands into his pockets.

Behind him he heard voices and turned around to see the two officers, who had walked closer to him.

"The temperature has dropped again," one said. "Before the sun has even set."

"Yes. I can smell the ice," his companion replied.

"How's that?"

"Haven't you heard? The wireless has been getting messages that we're headed toward some ice fields."

"Ice fields! Does the captain know?"

"Yes, he's changed course. Farther south and west. See where the sun is now?"

"Well, why hasn't he slowed down? Seems to me the engines are going faster."

"It's that Ismay hotshot."

Albert's ears pricked up. J. Bruce Ismay, he knew, was president of the White Star Line. He had taken one of the two fanciest suites in first class for the maiden crossing of the ship.

"He keeps barking orders at everyone," the officer was saying. "Wants to set a crossing record. Told Captain to go full steam ahead."

"Full steam ahead! Into *ice fields*?"

"Crazy, isn't it?"

"Crazy is putting it mildly. Suicidal's more like it."

The officers' voices faded as they walked to the door. Albert hugged his arms across his chest as he watched them leave, hurrying them in his mind.

Ice fields, he wondered. Where had he heard about ice fields?

Oh, yes. He remembered the conversation he'd overheard right here on this boat deck, as the ship left South-ampton the first day. The woman who predicted the *Titanic* wouldn't have enough lifeboats had told her friend what happened to the "unsinkable ship," the *Titan*, in the novel she'd read. "She set sail in April, just like we're doing, and she sank in the ice fields in the middle of the Atlantic."

Well, Albert wasn't going to be daunted by anything as unscientific as a novel. The air was too calm, the sky too beautiful. While he'd been looking the other way, the sun had begun sinking on the horizon, and the western sky blazed pink and red and orange, as brilliant as Grand-mother's gladiolus bed that Abraham nurtured every summer.

And what was the old poem Mattie Lou had taught him? *Red skies at night, sailor's delight. . . .*

Albert suddenly heard laughter. A whole cluster of peo-ple had congregated on the boat deck to go for a walk in the sunset.

Oh, for heck's sake, he thought with frustration. How long will *they* be up here? He pulled Father's watch from his pocket and looked at the time: 7:14. Darn! Mother would be worried. He'd promised to be back fourteen minutes ago.

Well, he'd have to get through one of the ship's barriers tomorrow. At least he still had three more days to find Harry Gordon.

Fifteen

Sunday, April 14, 1912.   11:10 P.M.

"Miss Harcher!" called Virginia.

Albert woke up with a start.

"Miss Harcher!" she cried again.

Albert sat up, remembering where he was. Mother's cabin. Uncle Clay had asked him to stay with Virginia while the grown-ups discussed family matters in the cabin Uncle Clay and Albert shared. Albert pushed the heavy overcoat he'd been using for a blanket to one side and turned on the light above the sofa. "You're all right," he assured his sister as he walked toward the brass double bed.

"Oh, Albert, it's only you."

"Yes. You must have been dreaming."

"I don't want it to be a dream. I want it to be true."

"What did you dream?"

"I dreamed that Miss Harcher was waiting for us in America."

"That's nice," he said dully. "Now close your eyes and go back to sleep."

"Do you think she'll be there?" Ginny pleaded.

"No. The *Titanic* was the only ship sailing from England this week. There wasn't enough coal for another one."

Virginia's voice grew shrill. "I want her to be waiting!"

Albert rolled his eyes. "Listen, Ginny. She won't be there. All her friends and family live in England. Close your eyes and go to sleep. Maybe you'll dream about her again."

"No!"

"Stop screaming. You'll wake the whole ship. Go back to sleep."

"*I can't sleep. My stomach hurts! I have 'pendicitis!*"

Good grief! Albert thought. People would start banging the cabin door if he didn't get her quiet. He shifted his weight, wondering what to do. "Look, I'll go find Mother. Try to relax. I'll be back in a minute."

No sooner had he opened the door than he heard the yelling from his own cabin.

"Do you really think Mama would stand by and let you disgrace her by becoming an actress?"

"Why would it disgrace her? Just tell me that. Why?"

"You know as well as I do. Actresses are cheap. Tawdry."

"That's not true! My friend, Zora LaRue—"

"Your friend Zora LaRue is a *suffragette*."

Nervously Albert reached in his pocket and clutched

Father's watch, not knowing if he should knock on the door.

"There's nothing wrong with women trying to get the right to vote!" Mother screamed. "We're human beings, you know! With brains! And feelings!"

"Let me tell you something else, Katherine. You know that director Zora LaRue arranged for you to try out with? Well, I made it a point to go meet him when I was in London. He said you were undoubtedly pretty once, but you're getting a bit long in the tooth to start an acting career now. And you don't have a thimbleful of talent."

Albert felt himself shaking. His heart was thumping in his chest. Afraid to hear any more, he turned around and hurried back to Mother's cabin.

Amazingly, Virginia had fallen asleep. He sat on the edge of the sofa, rocking back and forth as he listened to her soft, furry snoring. He needed to get out of here. He needed fresh air.

He'd go to the boat deck, he decided.

He knew it would be cold outside—freezing—so he grabbed the things he'd need to stay warm. Overcoat. Cap. Muffler. Gloves. He turned out the light. Then, as quietly as he could, he opened the door and turned the lock before leaving. Aware that the elevator wouldn't be working this late at night, he dashed to the stairs and climbed them.

Outside, the stars hung yellow and full, like golden apples waiting to be picked. The sea was black and still as slate. Albert leaned against the starboard railing of the boat deck, his muffler wound about his ears and mouth. He felt numb.

How could Uncle Clay have told such terrible lies to Mother? He hadn't really talked to the director in London, had he? Was Mother really too old to become an actress? Didn't she really have any talent?

And if she couldn't become an actress, what would become of all of them? Would Albert ever go to a school where he would have friends and play sports like baseball? Would he ever be able to study art?

Suddenly Albert was aware of a huge shadow in the water, blocking out many of the stars. Some large gray thing, taller than the funnels on the ship, was passing the *Titanic* and vibrating the railing he was leaning on. Albert stood up straight. From below came a harsh sound as if someone were dragging a stick across an iron grating. The sensation lasted half a minute, possibly longer. Then the shadow was gone, and the grinding noise stopped.

What had it been? Albert looked off in the distance, but all he could see were the golden stars and the quiet ocean. Had the whole thing been his imagination?

No. All at once the huge smokestacks above his head sent off steam with a roar that cracked the starry silence. The engines stopped churning the steady rhythm that Albert had grown accustomed to over the past four days, and the great *Titanic* lay motionless in the water.

The noise overhead was deafening, but the absence of motion—the deathlike stillness—frightened Albert even more. He stood paralyzed, squinting to see where the gray shadow might have gone.

An elderly gentleman rushed from the stairway and approached Albert. "What happened? Did you see?" he shouted. Albert could barely hear him with all the noise the smokestacks were making.

"We passed something in the water."

The man cupped his ear with a hand. "Eh?"

"We passed something in the water," Albert repeated louder.

"What was it?"

"I don't know. It was big, though. And gray. Like a shadow."

"I thought we were in an earthquake. My clothes started swaying on their hangers."

"It wasn't an earthquake."

"Eh?" the man said.

"It wasn't an earthquake," Albert yelled.

"How can you be sure?"

"Look how calm the water is."

"Glory be!" said the man. "I've crossed the Atlantic five times, and I've never seen the ocean that still."

Albert leaned on the railing again. The sea was a mirror, reflecting the stars so clearly he couldn't tell where the sky ended and the ocean began.

"I'm sure glad it wasn't an earthquake," the man shouted. "I was in the San Francisco earthquake in '06. Wharfside Saloon. Nearly got trampled to death."

"Trampled? How come?"

"Panic. People go crazy when they panic. Kill each other trying to save themselves."

The thought made Albert shudder.

"What do you think the shadow was that you saw?" the man asked.

Albert hesitated. Should he tell what he'd heard the officers discussing this afternoon—about the ice fields and Mr. Ismay's order to keep going full steam ahead? Would this man—would everyone on board—panic if they knew? He tried to keep his voice calm. "An iceberg, maybe."

"Eh?"

"An iceberg," Albert said more loudly.

"Glory be! That's why the engines stopped. The holds down below must be filling with water. I have to find my family."

Albert grabbed the man's arm. "The *Titanic* can't sink. I've read all about it. If one hold starts filling up, an automatic door closes so the water can't go anywhere else."

The man wriggled free. "Maybe so, but I'm not taking any chances. I'm going to get my family into good warm clothing. Get everyone into lifeboats before the panic starts. Panic is worse than just plain drowning."

Albert watched the man head back toward the stairs, wondering if the old gentleman were overreacting or if what he said made sense. If this were an emergency—if the passengers found out there weren't enough lifeboats on board—would everyone panic?

But this wasn't an emergency, was it? If the ship were in serious trouble, wouldn't someone have sounded an alarm by now?

Still, the ship *had* stopped after she scraped by the iceberg—or shadow—or whatever it was. And the smokestacks were still screeching.

Could the *Titanic* really sink?

Sixteen

Albert headed to the cabins to find his family, stopping first in the second-class smoking room to see if anyone there knew more about the accident than he did.

A gray-haired gentleman was sitting alone in a wing chair, snoring loudly. A younger man with a handlebar mustache was quietly smoking a cigar, probably his last one for the night. Two others were playing cribbage.

Relieved by the calm atmosphere in the room, Albert let out a sigh. Then he walked over to read the notice on the smoking-room wall. The *Titanic* had traveled 546 miles from noon Saturday until noon Sunday. Well, that was pretty fast, he knew, but the ship wouldn't set the crossing records Mr. Ismay was planning on if the engines didn't get started up right away.

Albert's stomach began to feel as if a swarm of bees were trapped inside. He left the room and walked quickly around the second-class promenade of B Deck, looking for an officer or crewman. The promenade was empty, so Albert decided to look in the second-class library below. He returned to the stairs.

Something was wrong with them, he thought. They seemed level to the eye, but they weren't. Albert's feet fell forward at each step, not quite hitting them right. Was the ship tilting? The staircase seemed to be listing toward the starboard and bow. No, that wasn't possible, he told himself. His imagination must be playing tricks on him. Maybe he was sleepy.

Albert continued down.

When he reached the second-class library on C Deck, the clock over the fireplace suddenly struck. Albert counted twelve bongs. Midnight. That seemed to be the cue for the only patron in the room—he was reading at a table—to leave. He stood up and waved good night to the library steward, who was still taking care of his paperwork for the day.

At the doorway the man almost bumped into Albert.

"Oops! Sorry there, young fellow. Well, well, you're up rather late, aren't you?"

"Yessir. I'm on my way to my cabin."

The man looked at Albert's coat and muffler. "You haven't been on the boat deck, have you?"

"Uh—yessir."

"I say, you didn't see anything unusual up there a few minutes ago, did you? A strong wave hitting the boat or anything? Something felt rather strange in here. A vibration. My pen fell off the table."

"It wasn't a wave, sir. The water is still as a pond. But

the ship passed a big shadow in the ocean. I think maybe we hit an iceberg. It—" Albert sucked in his breath, wondering if he'd said too much. He wasn't positive he'd seen an iceberg, and he didn't want to be responsible for starting unnecessary excitement on board. "It couldn't be a very serious accident, though. The noise wasn't very loud," he added.

"Of course not. This ship is unsinkable. Well, you go to your cabin, lad, and go to sleep."

"Yessir."

As soon as the man headed toward the stairs, Albert turned and went the other way. He wanted to stop by C Deck promenade to look for an officer.

No one was on the promenade except for a young couple strolling peacefully hand in hand. Albert relaxed, certain that the *Titanic*'s engines would start up at any moment.

But why didn't they?

Albert hurried back to the staircase and started down, again noticing that his feet didn't hit the steps properly, that his whole body seemed off balance. Three young men with dressing gowns cinched over their nightclothes were laughing and joking as they climbed toward him.

One of them held out a chunk of ice the size of a tennis ball toward Albert. "Look what just sailed through the porthole of our cabin. Bit of excitement, eh?"

If Albert had been uncertain before, that ice confirmed his worst fears. The swarming insects raced madly in his stomach.

"I'd say the ship just struck an iceberg, wouldn't you?" another man asked him, the tallest of the group.

Albert smelled alcohol and realized the men were tipsy. "Yes," he said.

"We're going up to the boat deck to see the fun. Want to come?" asked the third man with a nod of his head. He had an enormous handlebar mustache that brushed against Albert's cheek.

"I've just been there," said Albert. "There's not much to see right now."

"We want to take a look anyhow." The tall man's speech was fuzzy. "It's time something lively happened around here. The *Titanic* has too many rules for Sunday, if you ask me. No dancing, even. I'm ready for something lively."

"The clock just struck midnight," Albert said. "It's Monday now."

"Good thinking, boy, good thinking." The man with the mustache gave Albert a friendly pat on the arm. "Maybe something exciting will happen today."

"See you around," said the first man. The tall man waved.

Albert waved back and continued down the stairs, nodding to another cluster of passengers who were chatting together as they too headed toward the boat deck to find out why the ship had stalled. No one seemed concerned, merely eager for some kind of amusement after a dull Sunday night aboard the liner.

Turning at the pathway that led to the family's cabins, Albert wondered if Mother and Uncle Clay were still yelling at each other. He sure hoped not. He stood outside the cabin he shared with Uncle Clay, listening for loud voices. Nothing. The argument seemed to be over. Had Mother gone back to her own cabin? Was she asleep?

Well, he must wake her and tell her about the iceberg. He walked to her cabin and knocked on the door.

No answer.

He knocked again.

No answer.

He knocked a third time, much louder.

When there was still no answer, he tried the door. Locked. And he had no key. Why had he locked Mother's cabin when he left it?

He had a key to his own cabin, so he went back to that door again. He knocked, waited, then unlocked the door and turned on the light.

The room was empty, and the bunk beds hadn't been touched. Where were Mother and Uncle Clay? Was Mother asleep back in her own room with Virginia? Why hadn't she heard him knock?

Even if Mother were in her own room, where was Uncle Clay? He couldn't be off reading or playing bridge this time of night. Had the two of them heard the scraping noise and rushed to the boat deck to see what had caused it? If so, why hadn't Albert encountered them on his way down the stairs?

He took off his gloves, stuffed them into his pocket, and started toward the wardrobe to hang up his coat. But before he got there, he noticed a sheet of paper on the night table, a note:

Albert—

Your mother has disappeared. I think she's gone to the third-class area to talk to someone she met in London. Stay with V. until I find K. and bring her back.

C.T.

Albert reread the note, hoping he'd made a mistake the first time through. Despite his earlier envy of the people riding in third class, he knew that their area of the ship was the most dangerous to be in right now. If Mother's friend (Anna Skaggs, was it?) were assigned to a third-class cabin in the stern, Mother would have to climb four or five flights of stairs in the high-heeled slippers she'd been wearing to reach the open deck. But if Miss Skaggs were assigned to a cabin in the bow, Mother would have to walk the full length of the ship besides. And even if Mother reached the third-class poop deck before the *Titanic* settled too low in the water, she wouldn't find any lifeboats when she got there!

Without even feeling the pain, Albert bit his finger until he tasted blood. Oh, no! Not now, he thought.

As he reached for a handkerchief in his pocket to stop the bleeding, a new worry suddenly hit him. Something even worse.

He had locked Virginia alone in her cabin. And he didn't have a key.

Seventeen

Bam! Bam! Bam! Someone was pounding on the door.

"Uncle Clay?" Albert called. "Is that you?"

"It's me. Georgie. Open up."

Albert opened the door and looked out. The steward was wearing a coat and lifejacket over his nightshirt. His hair looked as if it had been stirred with a fork. "Captain's ordered folks to the top deck for a boat drill. Nothing what's to fret about, but all passengers and crew are to put on their lifejackets and report up above."

Did Georgie really believe this was just a drill? Albert wondered. Had the captain told the crew it was a drill in order to avoid panic? Albert's voice came out in a raspy sound he didn't recognize. "Have you—" He cleared his throat and tried again. "Have you seen Mother and Uncle Clay?"

"Can't say as I've seen any of your folks since just past lunchtime."

Squeezing his eyes tight for an instant, Albert let out a windy sigh. "Do you have your keys?"

"Yessir. I always carry me keys."

"You better let me into Mother's cabin. Virginia—Virginia may be locked in there alone."

Georgie nodded cheerfully. "Well now. We best be waking her, hadn't we? Captain wants everyone to the drill. Especially the little ones."

"Ginny?" Albert called softly as the door opened.

"Miss Virginia?" Georgie called louder.

The only response was the soft, animallike sound of his sister's snoring. Albert turned on the light, and the bedsprings squeaked eerily as Virginia rolled over.

Until now Albert had hoped that Uncle Clay's note had been wrong, that Mother was in her cabin with Virginia. He grabbed Georgie's arm. "Are you sure you haven't seen Mother or Uncle Clay since lunchtime?"

"Not since your mum stopped me in the pathway to ask for a needle and thread. Said you'd torn your pocket and hadn't bothered to tell her about it."

Albert's finger was throbbing. He'd wrapped the handkerchief too tight around his wound. "I—I think maybe she went to see someone she knows in third class," he said, unloosening the makeshift bandage. "Uncle Clay too. If they're down there, will someone tell them about the boat drill?"

"Don't see why not," Georgie said calmly. "All stewards was told to wake their passengers."

"But Mother and Uncle Clay aren't passengers there! You're their steward!"

Georgie shrugged. "They likely ran into some other steward who already told them about the drill and are waiting above right this minute for you and your little one. Anyways, you don't have time to fret about such things now. Dress warmly now. Your sister too. And don't forget your lifejackets. I've got to wake me other passengers." Georgie headed for the open door as if boat drills were common in the middle of the night. As if the ship's engines hadn't died.

Albert sank into the wicker chair beside the bed and pressed his hands against his forehead. After a while he pulled Father's watch from his pocket and clenched it with both hands. What should he do? Sit here and wait in Mother's cabin in hopes that she and Uncle Clay would return? Or wake up Virginia and take her to the boat deck, just the two of them?

He opened the cover to the watch and read the time: 12:22.

What would Father do if he were here?

Albert realized he knew the answer to that question. Putting the watch back in his pocket, he stood and walked deliberately to his own cabin to find his lifejacket. When he returned, he leaned over his sister's bed. "Ginny, time to wake up."

Virginia stirred without opening her eyes.

He shook her gently. "Wake up."

Her eyes shut, she moaned softly and wiped at her face as if shooing a fly.

"Virginia," he said sternly, "sit up."

"Go away," she whined.

"I'm sorry, but you have to get dressed. We're going up to the boat deck to play a game."

"No."

"You have to. The captain said that everyone has to play. Sit up and I'll help you get dressed."

"I don't want to." She still hadn't opened her eyes.

"It will be fun. We're going to get in rowboats, like the ones on the Potomac. Remember them?"

"No."

"Sit up." He pulled her shoulders roughly. "You have to."

Sighing, she opened her eyes. "Can I take Elizabeth?"

Albert hesitated. "Yes, you can take your doll."

She sat still then while he helped her into stockings and shoes. Her flannel nightgown was probably warmer than a dress, so he didn't change that. But he put a sweater on her and then her coat, hat, and mittens. He wound a muffler around her head to keep the hat in place. Then he rewound his own muffler and strapped a lifebelt on each of them.

Was that all? Had he forgotten anything?

Yes. He must leave a message for Mother. He found a pencil and paper:

Dear Mother,

I've taken V. to the boat deck for the drill. I hope you're all right. I hope we see each other again.

I love you,
Albert

P.S. It isn't a drill. I saw the iceberg in the water and a piece of ice on the ship. The Titanic *is sinking.*

Leaving the light on and smoothing the covers, Albert lay the note on the bed where Mother would be sure to find it. After one final look around the room, he put on his gloves, took Virginia by the hand, and opened the door.

The pathways were more crowded than they'd been when he'd returned from the boat deck a few minutes earlier. Just ahead was a honeymoon couple—Mr. and Mrs. Dreyfus—who sat near his family in the dining saloon. They both wore silk dressing gowns over their nightclothes. Mrs. Dreyfus had flimsy bedroom slippers on her feet, but Mr. Dreyfus was barefoot.

"You should go back for your shoes," Albert told them. "And heavy coats. I've just been on the boat deck. It's really cold up there. Freezing."

Mr. Dreyfus looked at his wife with a giggle. "Oh we won't be up there long enough to get cold."

You'll be cold before you're warm again, Albert thought. If you're ever warm again.

Eighteen

As Albert opened the door to the boat deck, Virginia let go of his hand and pulled back. "What's that noise?"

Until he heard it again, Albert had forgotten about the ear-splitting sound of steam escaping from the row of huge funnels, like an attack of metal dragons. So far his sister hadn't cried for Mother, but this noise might just set her off. What would he do if Virginia started screaming to go back to the cabin? "I don't know, Ginny. Maybe it's part of the game we're going to play."

She nodded and whispered to the doll cradled in her left arm. "Don't worry, Elizabeth. It's just part of the game." But she reached for Albert's hand with her own right one and held it tight.

Albert led her onto the frigid boat deck, where scores of people had gathered in the time since he'd left it. It was a strange-looking crowd in all manner of dress. Some ladies wore dinner gowns and dainty evening slippers with coarse steamer rugs draped over their shoulders. Some wore bathrobes over their nightclothes and carried satchels containing their belongings. Others wore woolen motor coats and gloves, with scarves holding their broad-brimmed touring hats in place.

Except for officers and crewmen, the faces were those of familiar-looking second-class passengers, people Albert had noticed in the dining saloon or on the various promenades. Apparently the barriers between the class areas of the ship hadn't been removed and third-class passengers would have to go to the poop deck, where there weren't any lifeboats. He shivered thinking about it and about Mother in her blue dinner gown with no outer wrap for warmth.

"Why isn't Mum playing the game?" Virginia asked.

"Well—" Albert's lips stuck to his teeth as he tried to smile. "I guess she's playing it somewhere else on the ship."

"I want to play the game with Mummy."

Albert took a deep breath. "There isn't room on the ship for everyone to play in the same place. Mother and Uncle Claybourne are playing somewhere else."

"I want Mummy!"

So do I, he wanted to say. *I'm more worried about her than you are.* But he couldn't risk saying anything that would upset his sister. "You and I get to play the game together. Won't that be fun?"

"Promise?"

"I promise. Look, the crew is getting a lifeboat ready so we can play."

He held Ginny's hand as crew members prepared a lifeboat for lowering. The officer in charge seemed uncertain of what he was doing and changed his instructions several times, but in due course the crew removed the cover, then loaded the boat with lanterns, biscuits, water bottles, and rope.

Fascinated by what was going on, Virginia forgot about Mother and loosened her grip on Albert's hand. "It's a big boat," she said.

"Yes," he agreed. "Lots bigger than the rowboats on the Potomac."

The officer ordered the crewmen to crank the pulleys, and slowly the creaking davits swung outward until the boat hung clear of the ship's deck. A huge distance separated the edge of the boat deck and the suspended lifeboat, a gaping chasm over black waters eleven stories below. Albert understood why the boats had to be extended so far out—so they would clear the lower decks, which were wider. But he wondered how women dressed in hobble skirts and high heels could possibly jump that distance. And how could he ever lift Virginia into the boat?

All at once the deck was silent. Someone had shut off whatever engines below were causing the escape of steam through the overhead funnels, and the crowd was too startled to speak. People stared blankly at each other. The noise, terrible as it had been, had suggested the crew below was still trying to get the *Titanic* moving again. But what did the silence mean?

Then from somewhere in the first-class section of the ship came a new sound—a jolly one. An orchestra comprised of piano and strings was playing a lively dance tune.

"The Turkey Trot!" exclaimed a young man whom Albert recognized as the one he'd met earlier on the stairs carrying a piece of ice. Drunkenly, the man grabbed a partner as other people stood back to make room for the performers. Another tipsy couple joined in. All four dancers seemed to be having a great time, but some of the onlookers frowned.

One woman shook her head disapprovingly. "At a time like this!"

"On a Sunday too!" complained another passenger.

Albert didn't bother to remind them that it was Monday now. He had other worries. Why would the ship's musicians, who up until this evening had played only hymns and chamber music, suddenly strike up ragtime? Albert had a strange feeling that none of what he saw or heard was real, that he wasn't actually a part of what was going on. He felt like a viewer at a Nickelodeon, watching the fast-moving images on the screen as he listened to music from the pit.

Oblivious to the dancers, Mr. and Mrs. Dreyfus stood at the edge of the crowd, clinging to each other for comfort and warmth.

Virginia spotted them. "You didn't put your shoes on," she scolded Mr. Dreyfus. "You'll catch cold."

Mrs. Dreyfus stared open-mouthed at Ginny, then began laughing hysterically.

"Stop it," her husband said, shaking her. "This is no time to lose your wits."

"I didn't say anything funny," Virginia complained to Albert. "He *will* catch cold if he doesn't wear shoes, won't he? Mummy says so."

Before Albert could answer, a great swishing sound caught everyone's attention. A blue-white flash soared from the officers' bridge at the fore part of the ship to the starry sky high above the funnels. Stopping in midair, it exploded with a faraway blast and dropped a shower of lazy sparks to the black water below.

The bright light of the rocket revealed a smile on Virginia's upturned face. "I say, Bertie. I like this game. It's just like the Fourth of July."

"Um-hum." Albert did his best to smile back, but of all the things that had happened tonight, this one frightened him the most. He'd read about rockets at sea and knew they were used as a last desperate signal for rescue. Had the *Titanic*'s wireless failed to get a response? Were there any ships close enough to see this bright blue plea for help?

Nineteen

"Boat is ready for boarding," called the officer who had supervised its preparation. "Women and children only." One crewman was standing in the boat and another was standing on the gunwale to help the passengers across the terrifying open space.

Just as Albert started to lead Virginia toward the line of women and children waiting to board, he saw Colonel and Mrs. John Jacob Astor walk by. That meant the gates between first and second class had been unlocked, and people were moving freely about. Somehow that gave Albert hope about encountering Mother and Uncle Claybourne.

"Are all the barriers down now?" he asked a crewman.

"Don't know," the man barked. "I've got boats to load."

Albert approached a lady in an exquisite fur wrap and asked the same question.

"The ones on the boat deck are down," she said. "Everyone has access now between first and second class."

"What about third class?" Albert pleaded. "Have you seen any of those passengers?"

Still holding her brother's hand, Virginia tugged it for attention. "Come on, Bertie. We can play the game now."

The lady had walked away without answering Albert's question, but he felt more hopeful now that it was just a matter of time until Mother and Uncle Claybourne reached the boat deck. He decided to keep his sister where they were for a while longer to wait for them. "Oh, we don't want to be rude, Ginny. Let's let someone else have the first turn."

Albert and his sister watched as the crewmen helped two women across the wide chasm into the boat.

Once again the officer in charge cupped his hands. "Women and children!"

Virginia let go of Albert's hand and yanked fiercely at his arm. "It's our turn now. I want to go."

"Not yet," Albert whispered.

The crewmen helped several more passengers into the boat.

"Any women and children?" the officer shouted.

"Yes, yes!" called Mr. Dreyfus. "My wife here. Help her, please."

"No, Manny!" she screamed. "I won't go without you!"

"Yes, dearest. You must."

"I won't!" She clung to him.

"Madam, you're wasting time. Get in now," ordered the officer.

Mr. Dreyfus swept his wife off her feet and carried her forward. The officer took her in his arms and then handed her to the crewman on board the boat.

She reached out across the yawning gulf. "No! No!"

"Any more women and children?" called the officer. When none responded, he ordered four of his crewmen to climb aboard the lifeboat to man the oars. Then he signaled for the boat to be lowered, and it creaked slowly down to the inky ocean. Watching from above, Albert could see that the boat was less than three-fourths full.

Less than three-fourths full! Albert was sure there weren't enough lifeboats to accommodate all the liner's passengers, yet this one was being lowered already. Didn't the officer know what it would mean if all the boats were put to sea only partially filled? Albert had thought that he had a good reason for not boarding promptly, but now he felt guilty for wasting valuable space.

He seized Virginia's hand and hurried to another boat.

The officer in charge of loading this second boat was younger than the first one, but he seemed more confident, yelling and swearing at his crewmen in a Welsh accent. Albert had seen that face before and suddenly remembered where. The man was Fifth Officer Lowe, who had interrupted their conversation with the seaman the day that Emily and Albert had been sketching on the boat deck. "Lowe's a tough one, he is," the seaman had said, and now Albert agreed. This was the sort of man you'd want to be lost with, if you had to be lost.

"Ready for boarding," Officer Lowe called. "Women and children only."

Pushing Virginia in front of him, Albert got in line behind several women. When it was Ginny's turn, he handed her up to a crewman standing on the gunwale, and the sailor easily passed her to another man standing in the boat.

"Come on, Bertie," Ginny called to him.

Albert took a step forward, but Lowe held out an arm. "Where do you think you're going?"

"To board, sir. With my sister."

Lowe looked down at Albert's long trousers. "How old are you?"

"Thirteen."

"Bertie!" Virginia called. "Come play the game with me!"

"Move back," the officer told Albert. "The lifeboats is for women and children only."

"Please, sir. My sister is only six. Our mother—" Albert's voice broke. He hated it for breaking in front of this stern, deep-voiced officer. He swallowed. "I can't find my mother, sir, and—and I can't send my sister alone. She's only six years old. Please let me go with her."

"Well, she's all right to come. But those in long pants should act like men. Now move back."

"*Bertie!*" Ginny wailed. "*You promised!*"

"It's all right, Albert," said a familiar chirpy voice. "I'll take care of her."

He was startled to see Emily standing at his side. In his anxiety about Mother and Virginia, he'd forgotten about the Brewers. "Where's your family?" he asked.

She nodded toward the other side of the deck. "They boarded a boat over there. It left a few minutes ago."

"Why aren't you with them?"

"The boat was overcrowded, and the officer said someone would have to get off. I volunteered."

Albert stared at her. She had volunteered to get off a boat, to leave her family, while Albert had begged to enter one, not just so he could take care of Virginia, but so he would be safe too. He felt ashamed. "I—I'd be grateful if you'd take care of Ginny. I've told her we're just playing. She'll be all right if she thinks it's a game."

Emily nodded. "Yes."

"Hurry now," Albert said.

"Yes, step lively," said Officer Lowe. "We've no time for lollygagging."

Emily waved back to Albert, and the crewmen helped her across the gap. Behind her followed more women and finally the two sailors who were assigned to be in charge of the boat. The ship seemed to be running out of experienced seamen who knew how to row a lifeboat or handle a tiller. "Take her down," Lowe ordered.

As the boat creaked slowly down, Albert bit his lip. "Good-bye, Ginny. Enjoy the game. Good-bye, Emily." He refused to cry.

Twenty

Monday, April 15, 1912. 1:40 A.M.

Albert stared over the railing as Virginia's boat reached the bleak ocean below. But he couldn't make out Ginny's form, or Emily's, and it was too cold to stand here any longer in one spot.

He had to keep his blood circulating. He turned around and began pacing, searching for Mother and Uncle Claybourne.

With each passing minute he grew more certain that they weren't anywhere on the boat deck or on A Deck below. But was that a good sign or a bad one? Had they escaped in one of the early boats to be launched? Had they been trapped somewhere in the third-class section of the liner? What could have happened to them?

It was all his fault. He was being punished for being impatient with Ginny. For wanting to get even when she broke Father's watch. For never understanding that she was just a child. For hating London and Miss Harcher and never doing his lessons. Everyone on the *Titanic*—Mother, Ginny, Uncle Clay, the Brewers, Mr. and Mrs. Dreyfus, all these people he passed—was being punished too, because of Albert.

In the gymnasium he saw Colonel and Mrs. Astor, both wearing bulky white lifejackets and sitting on two dead-still mechanical camels. Pocketknife in hand, Colonel Astor was slicing a third lifejacket apart and showing his wife what it looked like inside.

Farther along Albert passed a group of bellboys not much older than he was, puffing on lighted cigarettes. They were making fun of the officers and joking about the current confusion aboard the ship that gave boys the chance to smoke while they were supposedly on duty.

Other groups of people were more somber. In one section of the boat deck about a hundred people had knelt together in prayer as Father Byles, a priest traveling second class, passed among them for confessions.

But the musicians, who had moved to the open boat deck from their earlier location inside the first-class lounge, continued their cheerful ragtime tunes as if it were a holiday evening in July on the banks of the Potomac.

A group of passengers was huddled together, watching one of the few remaining boats to be loaded, and Albert hurried over to see if Mother might be among them. Even though most of the boats had been launched, many women stood back, reluctant to leave the *Titanic* without their husbands or brothers or fathers.

A tall man came charging up. Clean shaven, he was about the same age as Uncle Clay, but something about his manner made him seem more forceful. "Ladies, you must get in at once. There isn't a minute to lose. You can't afford to pick and choose your boat. Don't hesitate. Take your children and get in. Get in."

Albert felt someone else pushing him from behind. "Yes, son. Hurry up now and do as Mr. Andrews says. He helped design this ship, you know. Get in the boat."

Turning around to face the second speaker, Albert saw a distinguished gentleman in his late fifties. "I—I'm thirteen, sir."

"Yes, yes. Well, get in the boat. No time to waste." The man was wearing a bowler hat and a brown cashmere coat with a velvet collar.

"I'm too old." Albert waved vaguely in the direction where Ginny had boarded with Emily. "The officer over there told me to act like—He told me I was too old."

"Thirteen? Of course you're not too old. I'll speak to the officer with this boat and get you on board."

The man tried to elbow forward, but Albert grabbed his arm. "No! Please, sir! Thank you, anyway. But I think I'd like—" Albert blinked back the tears that were forming in his eyes. "I'd like to be a man."

The man squeezed his eyes shut, and when he opened them, he seemed to have tears too. "Of course you would. I'm sorry I treated you like a child. What's your name, son?"

"Albert. Albert Trask."

"Where do you live?"

"Washington, D.C."

"Well, I'm proud to meet you, Albert Trask of Washington, D.C. I'll remember you. And if you ever get to New York—if we both ever get there—I hope you'll look me up." The man held out a hand to shake Albert's. Then he reached inside a pocket, fumbled with a few of his cards, and extended one. With a faint smile he turned and walked away.

Albert found a spot on the deck where it was light enough to read. He held up the card:

HARRY GORDON
Theatrical Productions
New York, New York

Twenty-one

"Everyone to the starboard side to straighten her up!" an officer shouted.

Although she had formerly tilted slightly starboard, the ship now rested much lower in the water and listed so steeply toward port that it seemed the ocean might wash over that side of the deck at any moment.

Scores of passengers rushed to obey the officer's command, and the deck beneath them settled back to a more even keel. Most of them also headed to the back of the ship, which appeared to be safer than the low-lying bow. But once Albert reached the starboard side, he saw a knot of passengers around the most forward davit in the first-class area. Earlier he had seen a small lifeboat launched from this spot, but now a collapsible boat was being set up in its place. With the ship listing so badly toward port, he wondered if it were possible to launch any more boats from starboard. Anxiously he joined the crowd that had already gathered to watch what was going on.

A small cluster of men whispered together.

"Is this the last boat, then?" one of them asked.

The last boat? Albert's heart pounded so hard he was afraid people standing nearby could hear it. He clutched his arms across his chest.

"I think there might still be one or two boats in the second-class area aft," someone else said.

"There are two more collapsibles on top of the officers' quarters. Officer Lightoller's up there right now trying to get them ready."

"I saw him earlier, working so hard the sweat rolled down his face. He took his coat off, even."

Albert shivered just thinking about going coatless in this air. His own nose felt numb from the cold.

"Lightoller's crazy. He'll never get any more collapsibles assembled and into the water before the ship goes down."

"I say we make a run for this boat here," someone whispered.

"Righto."

Two men rushed forward, then dozens more. Panic began. Albert felt himself crushed from all directions as the mob elbowed and swore. A woman screamed as she was knocked to the ground and stepped on. Three men successfully jumped into the boat, but an officer fired two warning shots into the air. "Get out of there! Clear out!" he shouted. "Women and children first."

Other passengers came to the aid of the officers. They pulled the injured woman to her feet and helped remove the jumpers from the lifeboat. Albert stood panting. The only way now to avoid being trampled—or accidentally shot—was to stay clear of any boats that might not yet be launched.

Smelling the stench of fear around him, Albert pushed his way through the mob, then studied the deck for the safest place to go. The stern, which was now elevated far above the bow, would be the last part of the ship to go under water. But there were too many people back there, several hundred at least. Any little problem could set off mass panic.

The musicians were now playing somber music. Hymns. They seemed to know that everyone on the ship was going to die. The musicians. The people crowded together on the stern. The "buttons" with their cigarettes. All those people kneeling in prayer. Everyone.

Albert wondered how much time he had left. From beneath the bulky lifejacket he pulled out Father's watch and read the time: 2:05.

He slid the watch back under his lifejacket, frowning at the awkward white thing he was wearing. It would keep him afloat, maybe, but it wouldn't keep him alive. The temperature of the sea was surely less than thirty-two degrees Fahrenheit, lower than the freezing point of fresh water. How long could a person survive in ice? Thirty minutes? Forty?

Suddenly the officers' bridge at the bow of the ship dipped under the water. A few men standing near him dived into the sea, but most of the crowd instinctively ran toward safety at the stern, which was rising sharply into the air.

The bow dipped lower, and Albert couldn't even maintain his footing, let alone move up the slippery deck to

the stern. He heard men and women behind him screaming. But all at once the human sounds were muffled by
crashes and thuds and the sounds of splintering wood and
glass.

Albert was swept overboard in a turmoil of swirling ice
water.

Twenty-two

The cold felt like a thousand knives. Albert sputtered and flailed in the water, trying to escape the pain. It was the worst pain he'd ever felt, the worst he'd ever imagined. Then something—debris or some part of the ship itself —hit him on the head, and the pain was even worse.

Gasping, he continued to struggle. "Help me!" he cried, his voice lost in the chorus of other voices screaming for help. "Help me! Help me!" He yelled and thrashed, yelled and thrashed, until he was so tired he could no longer move or whisper.

Without warning, something caught his arm, and he heard a gentle voice. "This one's but a lad. Give me a hand to lift him into the boat."

"We're overcrowded as it is." Another voice. Husky. "We've no room for more. You'll get us all swamped."

"He won't take up much room, and his head's been hurt. Help me lift him now."

"Oh, all right. But it's your fault if we go under."

Something was lifting him. Davits? No, davits lift boats, not people. Albert wasn't thinking straight.

"There, lad. You'll make it. Can you give us a bit of help now? Lift your leg over the side."

Albert tried, but his leg wouldn't move. Why wouldn't his leg move?

Ah. On something solid now. Out of the water. Where? In a boat?

He felt something warm in his face. Someone's breath? Who was leaning over him? Why couldn't he see? Why wouldn't his eyes open?

"Take it easy, lad." Gentle voice. "Nasty bump you got there."

Bump? Who got bumped?

"Look at it, would you." Gentle voice again.

"Concussion, most likely, if you ask me." Husky voice.

"Concussion! I hadn't thought about that. Don't lie down, lad." Gentle voice. "Open your eyes, boy. If you have a concussion, you mustn't go to sleep. There, now. Lean against that board I've propped there. Over here, Walker. Help me support the lad a minute."

"Toss him over, I say. No sense swamping our boat with them what's going to die anyways."

"He isn't dying. No one's going to die."

Thud! Albert heard a noise. Were the men fighting?

No. A different noise. More like something being dropped. Or thrown. Something small. A pocketknife? A watch, maybe?

Yes. Father's watch. Virginia had thrown Father's watch. No! She mustn't! Father would blame Albert. Say he wasn't responsible. Say he couldn't take care of things.

Why had Virginia thrown the watch? Why didn't she want to go on the ship? What ship? Were they on a ship?

Was Father's watch broken?

Albert reached for the watch in his pocket, but his hand wouldn't move. Why wouldn't his hand move?

"You mustn't go to sleep if you've got a concussion, lad."

Where was Father's watch?

"Open your eyes and talk to me," said the man.

Yes, talk. Ask about the watch. Albert struggled to speak, but nothing came out.

Too tired. Too tired to talk or move. Too tired to think.

"Don't go to sleep."

Yes, sleep. That was what Albert wanted to do. Sleep.

Twenty-three

Monday, April 15, 1912.   7:40 A.M.

Albert shivered from the cold, but sun shone on his closed eyelids. He groaned, trying to open them. His head felt like a battlefield, and his mouth tasted like burned rubber.

"Well, hello there," said a pleasant female voice. "Can you open your eyes?"

Albert did for an instant, but the bright sun made his pain worse. "My head," he told her.

"Yes, you had a nasty bump. I wish you'd open your eyes, though. I'd like to look at them."

With effort Albert looked up at her. She was a woman about Mother's age with blue eyes and light brown hair.

"Mmm. Your pupils look good. No serious aftereffects, I'd say. Of course, Doctor will want to check you again."

"Doctor?" Albert asked.

"Ship's doctor," the woman explained. "He's the one who looked at you. You're on the Cunarder *Carpathia*. We have some passenger doctors on board too. They've all had their hands full looking after the sick and wounded. We picked up the *Titanic*'s lifeboats nearly four hours ago." Albert turned his head slightly, noticing that he was one of many people lying or sitting on the open deck. "You all went through a bit of something, I'd say," the woman added.

"Yes," Albert agreed.

"I'm Pauline Wimmer from Fargo, North Dakota. Not a registered nurse, but I've worked in a doctor's office back home, so I volunteered to help."

"I'm Albert Trask. Washington, D.C."

"Yes, I know."

She knew his name? That could only mean good news. "You've seen my mother? My family's all right?"

"Well, your sister's all right."

"Oh."

"Your friend is taking care of her," Miss Wimmer said.

"You mean Emily?"

"Yes, Emily. She's been very worried about you. She's been by every few minutes to check on you. She was here when Doctor looked you over. Tell me, can you wiggle your toes?"

Albert tried. His feet were numb inside his wet shoes. "Maybe. I—I'm not sure."

"We'll have to take those shoes off. Can you sit up?"

Albert tried to lean up on one elbow. It was hard to move under the weight of the steamer rug someone had placed over him. The very effort made the soldiers inside his skull brandish their rusty swords. "My head hurts."

"Of course it does. I should be more thoughtful. Doctor gave me some painkiller to give you if—when you woke up. I'll go get some water for you to take it with and some hot broth and toast. You try to sit up while I'm gone, and we'll get those shoes off when I come back."

She started off, and Albert struggled to a sitting position. He looked around him, seeing all the people on the deck. Most of them were bundled in steamer rugs as well as heavy coats, and they all seemed downcast and silent.

"Oh, Albert!" cried a familiar voice. "You're alive!" Albert looked up to see Emily standing over him. Her eyes were black hollows in cheeks the color of lint. "The doctor said you—" Emily put her hands over her face, suddenly sobbing. Emily Brewer, the brave girl who had volunteered to leave her family's lifeboat as the *Titanic* was about to sink, was crying. Over him.

"I'm fine," he told her. "Where's Virginia?"

"She's all right. She's with Mother."

"Your family's safe?"

"Yes." Emily sniffled, then wiped her eyes with the back of her hand. "We were really lucky. But Sarah's sick. Scarlet fever. A lady from Denver heard the doctor say that and gave us her cabin. Wasn't that nice? It's much warmer down there."

"Scarlet fever!" Albert exclaimed. "That's pretty serious, isn't it? And contagious?"

Emily nodded. "Robert and I both had it on the tramp steamer we took from Capetown. We hoped Sarah wasn't going to come down with it, but she's sicker than either one of us were. There's not enough antiseptic on this ship for the doctor to paint her throat, but he gave us a prescription for when we get to New York. You can see the blisters in her throat, so you know the pain is killing her, but she's too sick to cry or complain. Virginia can't understand why Sarah won't talk to her."

"Oh, I'm sorry!" he said. Then another thought occurred to him. "Virginia shouldn't stay in the cabin with her."

Emily shrugged. "The doctor said she might as well. She's already been exposed, and it's warmer down there. Besides, she didn't know anyone on this ship but us. We couldn't just leave her alone."

"Thank you for taking care of her. I really appreciate that. But I can do it now."

Emily crouched beside him. "I'll bring her in a minute, but I need to talk to you first. I—I have bad news, Albert. I don't think your mother and uncle made it. I've looked everywhere and asked everyone, but no one has seen them. And—and their names aren't on the list."

For a moment Albert was unable to speak. He closed his eyes, remembering the sketches he'd seen of the *Titanic*'s construction. He imagined the terror Mother must have gone through as she climbed the flights of stairs from the third-class bowels of the ship. "Have you—" His voice broke, and he had to try again. "Have you told Virginia?"

"No. I wanted to be sure."

"Bring her here so I can tell her, will you? I don't think I can walk yet."

"Yes!" Emily sprang to her feet, eager as always to be doing something for someone else. "I'll be right back. Don't go away."

Albert smiled wryly. There was no chance he'd go anywhere right now without help.

Miss Wimmer returned with his medicine and breakfast. After he'd eaten, she removed his shoes and examined his feet.

"Color looks pretty good," she told him. "I'm not a doctor, of course, but I think they'll be all right. You'll have a scar on your head, though, unless we're not too late for stitching. Doctor didn't want to waste time earlier doing that because he didn't know if you'd pull through the hypothermia. But I'd say you've done it. What do you think?"

"I feel lots better. Thanks."

"Is it all right if I go look at some other patients now?"

"Sure. I'll be fine. The food helped a lot."

"The painkiller will too, after it's had time to work. Well, I'll be back. Don't worry."

Emily returned then, holding Virginia by the hand. His sister still clutched her doll. Her face was blotchy, and she'd lost her hair ribbon.

"Oh, Ginny," he began, his voice breaking again. Darn it. He wasn't going to cry, was he? He wiped his eyes with the edge of the steamer rug. Albert held out his arms. "Come here, Ginny. Come on, please."

She walked close but stood stiff as a flagpole, allowing him to hug her for barely a second before she pulled away. "You promised you'd play the game with me."

"I'm sorry. The officer wouldn't let me."

Albert could taste the broth he'd just eaten and hoped he wasn't going to throw up. How could he explain to his sister what had happened to Mother and Uncle Claybourne when she was in this mood?

"Sit down next to me," Albert said. "I need to talk to you."

Virginia sat cross-legged, a few feet away. "You lied," she scolded. "You said it was a game."

"Yes, I did. I thought you'd be afraid to get in a lifeboat, and I didn't want you to be scared."

"I wasn't scared. I'm not a baby, am I, Elizabeth?" she asked the doll.

"I'm sorry I didn't tell you the truth. I thought I was doing the right thing. But we need to talk about something else now."

Emily's coat brushed his arm as she shifted her weight. "I'll go to the cabin while you talk. It's B 16. Send someone to get me if you need me."

"Yes," Albert said, only vaguely aware of her. He felt dizzy. His throat stung. How should he begin what he had to tell his sister?

He patted the wooden flooring beside him. "Sit closer, Ginny." He swallowed. "My throat hurts from yelling last night. It's hard for me to talk."

She frowned. "Everybody has a sore throat. Nobody wants to talk or play. I hate sore throats."

"Come on." He patted the deck again.

Ginny scooted a bit closer, pulling his steamer rug over her own lap and up to her doll's chin. "I'm so cold. The lifeboat was cold too. And there was a lady who yelled and yelled. About dying. It was awful, Bertie. It wasn't a game."

Albert sighed. "I'm sorry I treated you like a baby. But now I'm going to treat you like a big girl and tell you the truth. Can you act like a big girl?"

"I *am* a big girl. I'm six and a half. Sarah is only six."

"Yes, I know. That's why I'm going to tell you something important. Listen, Ginny. Dying isn't terrible. It's nothing to be afraid of. When people die, they go to a beautiful place called heaven where they'll never be cold again or sick or have any more pain."

"Mum says Papa's in heaven."

"Yes." Albert nodded. "He is."

"He isn't cold like I am? He never gets sore throats like Sarah's?"

"No."

The silence seemed to last forever as she bit her lip, considering that. "Then why did the lady on the boat yell so loud?"

"I guess she was frightened. People do silly things when they're frightened."

"I didn't yell," Virginia said.

"Wonderful. I'm proud of you for that."

"I sort of cried, though. I wasn't scared, but I was lonely. You didn't come with me like you promised. And Mum didn't either. Where is Mum?"

Albert cleared his throat. "That's what I wanted to tell you, Ginny. We're—we're never going to see Mother again. She and Uncle Clay have gone to heaven. To be with Father."

She turned toward him, her face contorted with anger. She kicked off the steamer rug. *"That's not fair!"* She pounded his chest with her fists. *"That's not fair! I need her more than Papa does!"*

Albert's chest ached. His head throbbed. But he didn't try to stop her fists. Let her hit me, he thought. Let her be angry. It was terrible when your parents died. When they deserted you. He knew how she felt.

She tired of hitting him and buried her face in her hands. Her body shook, but no sobs came out. No noise. Albert waited for her sobs. He waited for her to speak.

When she made no effort to say anything, he put his arm around her. "I know you need Mother, Ginny. I need her too. But we're lucky we still have each other. I'll take care of you now."

Suddenly she threw her arms around him. "Oh, Bertie!" she wailed. "Don't you ever go to heaven!"

"Not until you're lots, lots older, Ginny. I'll stay with you as long as you need me."

For a long time they held each other, their tears mingling on their wet cheeks. The doll caught between them poked Albert's side, but he didn't even bother to move it.

After a while, he realized someone was standing beside them and looked up.

"Well, Albert Trask," said a round-faced man carrying a doctor's satchel. "Miss Wimmer says you're getting strong as an ox. I think maybe I should give you a going-over and see if I agree with her. Now . . . you just sit where you are and try to relax."

"Yessir." Albert pulled a cold, soggy handkerchief from his pocket to wipe his own tears and then Ginny's.

"Well, girlie," the doctor said to Virginia when Albert had put the handkerchief away again. "I'm going to examine your brother now. Why don't you run off and play for a few minutes?"

"No," said Virginia.

The doctor looked stunned, so Albert tried to excuse his sister's bad manners. "She just found out that our mother and uncle—" He had to sniffle before he could continue. "That they were lost last night. Let her stay here. She needs to be with me right now."

"Oh, yes. I understand."

Virginia was talking to her doll. "We're lucky we still have each other, Elizabeth. Don't worry, Albert and I will take care of you."

Twenty-four

Wednesday, May 22, 1912.   8:40 P.M.

"No!" Virginia screamed. *"No! I won't let you! Take it away!"*

Albert laid the pencil on top of his sketch pad and hurried down the hall to his sister's room.

Dressed for the night, Ginny was sitting up in bed, her old doll clutched tightly in her arms as a new doll lay at her side. Grandmother stood at the bedside, leaning heavily on her cane and looking as fierce as a grizzly bear. Farther away, Mattie Lou wrung her hands.

When his sister saw him, she sprang out of bed and ran toward Albert. Her arm that wasn't holding Elizabeth hugged him around his waist. "Don't let her, Bertie! Tell her she can't!"

"What's going on?" Albert asked.

"I'm just trying to give her a new doll," Grandmother explained. "A much nicer one than Elizabeth."

"*She wants to burn Elizabeth!*" Ginny shrieked.

"How come?"

Grandmother sighed. "Doctor's orders. He says I have to burn all the books and playthings Virginia kept with her while she had scarlet fever. They're contagious now and can make other people sick."

Virginia looked up at him. "Not Elizabeth!" she wailed. "Don't let her, Bertie!"

"What other people?" Albert asked his grandmother. "Hardly anyone ever comes here. And all of us—Abraham too—were exposed to plenty of Virginia's germs while we were taking care of her. If we're going to get scarlet fever, we won't catch it from some little doll."

Without speaking, Mattie Lou nodded vigorously.

Albert took a deep breath, then went on in a low voice. "Elizabeth is all she has left, Grandmother. Everything else was lost on the ship. Her mother. Her toys. Her clothes. You even got rid of the clothes we were wearing. You can't burn the only thing in this world Virginia was able to save."

From under brows like wooly caterpillars, Grandmother looked icily at him, trying to stare him down. "This isn't your decision, young man. It's the doctor's. And mine."

Virginia's arm tightened around Albert's waist, giving him strength. "Yes, it *is* my decision," he said.

Grandmother gasped. He'd never defied her before. Maybe no one had ever stood up to her before, Albert thought. She raised her cane, and for a moment he was afraid she might strike him.

Albert's heart pounded, but he went on talking. "Before Father died, he left me in charge of Mother and Virginia.

Now that Mother's dead too, it's my job to take care of Ginny." He looked from Grandmother to Mattie Lou and back to Grandmother again to make sure they were listening. "The three of us and Abraham have already been exposed to scarlet fever, so we can touch Elizabeth if we need to. But Ginny can't take that doll anywhere outside our yard. And if any other children should come over to play, she'll have to put Elizabeth in her closet. The rest of the time she's free to play with any doll she chooses."

Grandmother scowled but slowly lowered her cane.

"Tomorrow," Albert continued, "I'll have Abraham drive me to the druggist's to buy some alcohol. When I get home I'll bathe Elizabeth with it. Then I'll wash and iron her clothes."

He stood silent, waiting for Grandmother to respond. When she didn't, Albert kissed his sister on the cheek. "Go to sleep now, Ginny. Everything will be all right," he said, with more confidence than he felt.

"Thank you, Bertie," she whispered and scooted back to bed.

Albert reached for Father's watch in his pocket and squeezed it tightly. He could scarcely believe he'd just spoken in that tone to his domineering grandmother, and he didn't know whether to be proud or ashamed or worried. Worry seemed to be his dominant emotion, though, so he turned on his heels to flee. But before he reached the door, he felt a hand on his shoulder. "It'll be my pleasure to bathe that dolly and her clothes," Mattie Lou said softly. "I believe I know more 'bout heating a flatiron on a coal stove than yourself."

He smiled his thanks and headed back to his room.

But his heart was still pounding. Winning Mattie Lou

to his side didn't necessarily mean that Grandmother was convinced. She might even be angrier than she was before. Maybe she was making plans right now to sneak off and burn Elizabeth in the middle of the night. And that probably didn't even compare to her plans for Albert in the morning.

He sat at his desk and picked up his art pencil, but he was too nervous to sketch any more. He tossed his pencil, stood up again, and started pacing.

He stopped.

Footsteps were coming down the hall. Grandmother was limping slowly toward his room with her cane. Albert rushed back to his chair and pretended to draw.

When she entered the room, he rose courteously, as Mother had taught him always to do for someone who was older. "Yes, ma'am?" he said, standing bravely, his shoulders back.

Grandmother motioned with her cane. "Sit down, Albert. You look as stiff as a mop handle." She pulled up another chair for herself and dropped weightily into it before resting an elbow on his desk and burying her eyes and thick brows under a broad hand. She sighed and moved her hand.

He waited.

"You'll make a good lawyer," she said at last.

That wasn't exactly what he thought she was going to say. In fact, it was so far from what he expected that he wondered if he'd heard correctly. "Pardon me?"

"A good litigator," she added. "A good addition to the firm. Your grandfather would be proud of you."

He still didn't understand. "Ma'am?"

"Your defense of that doll. It was very good."

"Thank you," he said, startled. Then suddenly he realized it *had* been a good defense, an excellent one. Grandmother hadn't even argued with him.

But of course he had no intention of becoming a lawyer, or joining the family firm. And this seemed to be as good a time as any to make Grandmother understand that. He took a deep breath. "I'm not going to be a lawyer, Grandmother. I want to be an artist."

Grandmother waved her hand in front of her face as if batting away a cobweb, and changed the subject. "I've sent for Miss Harcher," she said. "Her boat arrives next week."

"*Miss Harcher!*" Albert exclaimed.

"Yes, I knew I'd have to engage a tutor of one kind or another. And I thought your sister would have an easier adjustment—to things here—with a teacher she was already comfortable with. She's been through a lot for a six-year-old."

Albert squeezed his hands together in his lap. He hated to admit—even to himself—that Grandmother might know as much about Ginny's needs as he did, but it was true that his sister *would* feel comfortable with Miss Harcher. Even if the thought of his being penned up with that old she-goat again almost made him want to throw up.

"Miss Harcher was very pleased to hear from me," Grandmother continued. "It seems she's always wanted to emigrate to America. But I've had the feeling from your mother's letters that you didn't enjoy being tutored by her, that you'd prefer to go to a school."

Albert nodded. "Yes, ma'am."

"Your mother said you missed physical recreation. Sports."

"Yes, ma'am," he repeated.

"I'm sorry there aren't any schools nearby, Albert. But your uncle was thoughtful. Before he left for England, he went to the trouble of looking into a military boarding school he thought you might attend. I understand it has a very good basketball team."

Albert jumped to his feet. He wanted to make sure Grandmother heard him this time. And standing above her gave him an advantage he needed. "I know Uncle Claybourne thought I should attend military school before I went to law school. But I don't want to go to either one. I've decided to be an artist, or maybe an architect, not a lawyer."

"Oh, for heaven's sake, Albert! You're only thirteen years old. You're too young to decide on any career yet." She thumped the floor with her cane. "And sit down, will you? I can't talk to anyone who's lording over me like the Russian czar."

Albert returned to his chair. But only the very edge. "I mean it, Grandmother. I want to study art. They don't teach art in military school. Anyway, I can't leave Ginny. After the *Titanic* went down—after I told her that Mother had died—I promised Ginny that I wouldn't leave her until she was ready to have me go. I—I don't think she's ready yet."

"Then I don't suppose you'd be interested in the other school I had in mind either?"

"What other school?" Albert asked.

"Oh, give me credit, young man. I knew that uncle of

yours was overreacting to your interest in art. So I took the trouble to look into a school in Washington with a highly recommended art teacher. It's close enough so you could come home on weekends. And it has a better-than-average physical education program, even a swimming pool."

Albert sat back, digesting what he'd just heard.

Grandmother thumped the floor again. "Well then, how does that sound?"

It sounded magnificent. The answer to his dreams. But Albert couldn't leave Virginia just yet. What if she had another problem with Grandmother, like the one about the doll? "I'd like that a lot—in a year or two, maybe. Not yet. I can't break my promise to Ginny," he said softly.

The old lady pursed her lips together, studying the carpet. "I take it that means you'll make an effort to get along with Miss Harcher this time? That you'll do the lessons she assigns?"

Albert sighed. "Yes."

"You won't complain about your lack of friends?"

"No."

"And you'll get your physical activity by helping Abraham with his chores?"

Albert nodded. His grandmother had given him a new idea, a wonderful one. "How would it be if Abraham and I started by digging a hole for a swimming pool? I know we couldn't do all the work, but you could pay for the rest of it with money from the inheritance I'll get when I'm twenty-one."

"Hmm," said Grandmother.

Now that he had warmed to his subject, he spoke faster,

more confidently. "Virginia needs exercise too. And she should learn to swim. I realized when the ship went down that everyone should be able to swim. And swimming is something Ginny and I could do together."

"Hmm."

"Please, Grandmother?"

Leaning on her cane, Grandmother stood. "I was right about you, Albert."

Albert rose too. "Yes, ma'am?" he asked.

"You'll make a very good lawyer. Your grandfather would be proud."

As Albert listened to his grandmother's footsteps retreating down the hall, he felt both pleased and angry. Even though Grandmother understood his interest in art, she still expected him to be a lawyer. He knew he'd have to find a way to convince her that he was serious about becoming an artist.

But he'd kept his promise to Ginny. That was good enough for now, Albert decided. He sat down, opened his notepad to a fresh page, and began to sketch a swimming pool.

Author's Postscript

Titanic Crossing is a work of fiction based upon a real episode in history. Where I have used the names of actual people aboard the liner—Captain Edward J. Smith, J. Bruce Ismay, Second Officer Charles H. Lightoller, Fifth Officer Harold G. Lowe, Thomas Andrews, Colonel John Jacob Astor, and Mrs. Madeleine Astor—I have tried to record the events about them as accurately as possible.

Captain Smith, for instance, did (at the insistence of Ismay, the managing director of the White Star Line) order the *Titanic* to proceed at full speed late Sunday, April 14, 1912, even though the ship was approaching known ice fields. Furthermore, he failed to hold a boat drill early on during the voyage, an exercise which undoubtedly would have saved many additional lives. On the other hand, he acted wisely during the crisis by ordering the orchestra to play lighthearted tunes and in other ways acting calmly to prevent mass panic. Smith went down with the ship, and his body was never recovered.

Among the other officers, Lightoller and Lowe most distinguished themselves for their cool-headed decisions and vigorous actions during the emergency. Both these men survived the disaster, and Lightoller recorded his version of the sinking in a book entitled *Titanic and Other Ships*, which was first published in 1935.

Andrews, a designer of the ship, was one of the first people aboard to realize that the *Titanic* was doomed. As the lifeboats were being filled, he raced from one to another, ordering women and children to board them quickly. Unfortunately, not many people recognized who he was, and few took his warnings seriously. Andrews himself was one of the people who died in the icy water.

For his luxurious suite on the ship, multimillionaire Astor paid $4,350, or approximately $50,000 by today's standard. (By comparison, a third-class ticket was about $35.) He also flaunted his wealth by purchasing an $800 lace bed jacket for his wife from the merchants who boarded the *Titanic* at Queenstown, Ireland (now known as Cobh). Perhaps he thought his money would save him from the tragedy, but it did not. Nineteen-year-old Madeleine, however, did survive the experience. She lived to bear the son of Astor she was carrying at the time, and to marry and divorce two more husbands.

In addition to these persons I refer to in *Titanic Crossing*, several of the characters in the book were inspired by real people aboard the liner, but I have changed their names because the events I describe are fanciful. A famous theatrical producer named Henry B. Harris was traveling in first class, and he was my inspiration for Harry Gordon. Thirteen separate couples were honeymooning aboard the ship, and like my characters Mr. and Mrs. Dreyfus, many of them shared tearful farewells as the wives were admitted to the lifeboats without their new husbands. And twelve-year-old Ruth Becker, who was traveling home to America with her mother and two younger siblings, was the inspiration for Emily Brewer. Like Emily, Ruth was the daughter of missionaries, and she had a young brother in desperate need of medical treatment. But unlike Emily's, Ruth's father was alive in India.

Despite all the above, the provenance of *Titanic Crossing* came from a single episode I read about: a thirteen-year-old boy on the ship was at first prevented from boarding one of the lifeboats because he was considered a man. Somehow this incident struck me so deeply that I felt compelled to write a novel about it, though the character Albert Trask and all his relatives in my story arose from my own imagination.

Writing this book has been, in large part, a tribute to that actual young man. I hope he would not be displeased by my effort.

—Barbara Williams